D1086708

DOORWAYS IN
THE SAND

Roger Zelazny

This edition published in 2017 by Farrago,
an imprint of Prelude Books Ltd
13 Carrington Road, Richmond, TW10 5AA, United Kingdom

www.farragobooks.com

This work was originally published serially in *Analog Science Fiction/
Science Fact*

ISBN: 978-1-911440-87-1

To Isaac Asimov
with high regard,
deep respect,
and full fondness.

1

LYING, LEFT HAND FOR A PILLOW, on the shingled slant of the roof, there in the shade of the gable, staring at the cloud-curdles in afternoon's blue pool, I seemed to see, between blinks, above the campus and myself, an instant piece of skywriting.

DO YOU SMELL ME DED? I read.

A moment's appraisal and it was gone. I shrugged. I also sniffed at the small breeze that had decided but moments before to pass that way.

"Sorry," I mumbled to the supernatural journalist. "No special stinks."

I yawned then and stretched. I had been dozing, had regarded the tag end of a dream, I supposed. Probably just as well that I could not recall it. I glanced at my watch. It indicated that I was late for my appointment. But then, it could be wrong. In fact, it usually was.

I edged forward into a 45° hunker, my heels still resting against the ice-catching eyelets, my right hand now upon the gable. Five stories below me the Quad was a study in green and concrete, shade and sunlight, people in slow motion, a fountain like a phallus that had taken a charge of buckshot at its farther end. Beyond the fountain lay Jefferson Hall, and up on Jeff's third floor was the office of my latest adviser, Dennis Wexroth. I patted my hip pocket. The edge of my schedule card still jutted there. Good.

To go in, go down, go across and go up seemed an awful waste of time when I was already up. Although it was somewhat out of keeping with the grand old tradition as well as my personal practice to do much climbing before sundown, the way across—with all the buildings connected or extremely adjacent—was easy and reasonably inconspicuous.

I worked my way about the gable and over to the far eave. About three feet outward and six down, an easy jump, and I was on the library's flat roof and trotting. Across the roofs and about the chimneys on a row of converted townhouses then. Over the chapel, Quasimodo-like—a bit tricky there—along a ledge, down a drainpipe, another ledge, through the big oak tree and over to the final ledge. Excellent! I had saved six or seven minutes, I was certain.

And I felt most considerate as I peered in the window, for the clock on the wall showed me that I was three minutes early.

Wide-eyed, openmouthed, Dennis Wexroth's head rose from its reading angle, turned slowly, darkened then, continued upward, dragged the rest of him to his feet, about his desk, toward me.

I was looking back over my shoulder to see what he was glaring at when he heaved the window open and said, "Mister Cassidy, just what the hell are you doing?"

I turned back. He was gripping the sill as if it were very important to him and I had sought its removal.

"I was waiting to see you," I said. "I'm three minutes early for my appointment."

"Well, you can just go back down and come in the same way any . . ." he began. Then: "No! Wait!" he said. "That might make me an accomplice to something. Get in here!"

He stepped aside and I entered the room. I wiped my hand on my trousers, but he declined to take it.

He turned away, walked back to his desk, sat down.

"There is a rule against climbing around on the buildings," he said.

"Yes," I said, "but it's just a matter of form. They had to pass something as a disclaimer, that's all. Nobody pays any atten—"

"You," he said, shaking his head. "You are the reason for the rule. I may be new here, but I've done my homework so far as you are concerned."

"It's not really very important," I said. "So long as I'm discreet about it, nobody much cares—"

"Acrophilia!" he snorted, slapping the folder that lay on his desk. "You once bought a screwball medical opinion that saved you from being suspended, that even got you some sympathy, made you a minor celebrity. I just read it. It's a piece of garbage. I don't buy it. I don't even think it's funny."

I shrugged. "I like to climb things," I said. "I like to be up in high places. I never said it was funny, and Doctor Marko is not a screwball."

He emitted a labial consonant and began flipping through pages in the folder. I was beginning to feel a dislike for the man. Close-cut sandy hair, a neat, matching beard and mustache that almost hid his mean little mouth. Somewhere in his mid-twenties, I guessed. Here he was getting nasty and authoritarian and not even offering me a seat, and I was probably several years his senior and had taken pains to get there on time. I had met him only once before, briefly, at a party. He had been stoned at the time and considerably more congenial. Hadn't seen my file yet, of course. Still, that should make no difference. He should deal with me *de novo*, not on the basis of a lot of hearsay. But advisers come and go—general, departmental, special. I've dealt with the best and I've dealt with the worst. Offhand, I can't say who was my favorite. Maybe Merimee. Maybe Crawford. Merimee helped me head off a suspension action. A very decent fellow. Crawford almost tricked me into graduating, which would probably have gotten him the Adviser of the Year award. A good guy, nevertheless. Just a little too creative. Where are they now?

I drew up a chair and made myself comfortable, lighting a cigarette and using the wastebasket for an ashtray. He did not seem to notice but went on paging through the materials.

Several minutes passed in this fashion, then: "All right," he said, "I'm ready for you."

He looked up at me then and he smiled.

"This semester, Mister Cassidy, we are going to graduate you," he said.

I smiled back at him.

"That, Mister Wexroth, will be a cold day in hell," I said.

"I believe that I have been a little more thorough than my predecessors," he replied. "I take it you are up on all the university's regulations?"

"I go over them fairly regularly."

"I also assume you are aware of all the courses being offered this coming semester?"

"That's a safe assumption."

He withdrew a pipe and pouch from within his jacket, and he began loading the thing slowly, with great attention to each fleck and strand, seeming to relish the moment. I had had him pegged as a pipe smoker all along.

He bit it, lit it, puffed it, withdrew it and stared at me through the smoke.

"Then we've got you on a mandatory graduation," he said, "under the departmental major rule."

"But you haven't even seen my preregistration card."

"It doesn't matter. I've had every choice you could make, every possible combination of courses you might select to retain

10

your full-time status worked out by one of the computer people. I had all of these matched up with your rather extensive record, and in each instance I've come up with a way of getting rid of you. No matter what you select, you are going to complete a departmental major in something."

"Sounds as if you've been pretty thorough."

"I have."

"Mind if I ask why you are so eager to get rid of me?"

"Not at all," he replied. "The fact of the matter is, you are a drone."

"A drone?"

"A drone. You don't do anything but hang around."

"What's wrong with that?"

"You are a liability, a drain on the intellectual and emotional resources of the academic community."

"Crap," I observed. "I've published some pretty good papers."

"Precisely. You should be off teaching or doing research—with a couple degrees after your name—not filling a space some poor undergrad could be occupying."

I dismissed a mental picture of the poor would-be undergrad—lean, hollow-eyed, nose and fingertips pressed against the glass, his breath fogging it, slavering after the education I was denying him—and I said, "Crap again. Why do you really want to get rid of me?"

He stared at his pipe, almost thoughtfully, for a moment, then said, "When you get right down to basics, I just plain don't like you."

"But why? You hardly know me."

"I know *about* you—which is more than sufficient." He tapped my file. "It's all in there," he said. "You represent an attitude for which I have no respect."

"Would you mind being more specific?"

"All right," he said, turning the pages to one of many markers that protruded from the file. "According to the record, you have been an undergraduate here for—let me see—approximately thirteen years."

"That sounds about right."

"Full-time," he added.

"Yes, I've always been full-time."

"You entered the university at an early age. You were a precocious little fellow. Your grades have always been quite good."

"Thank you."

"That was not a compliment. It was an observation. Lots of grad material too, but always for undergrad credit. Quantity-wise, in fact, there is the substance of a couple of doctorates in here. Several composites suggest themselves—"

"Composites do not come under the departmental major rule."

"Yes. I am well aware of that. We are both quite well aware of that. It has become obvious over the years that your intention is to retain your full-time status but never to graduate."

"I never said that."

"An acknowledgment would be redundant, Mister Cassidy. The record speaks for itself. Once you had all the general requirements out of the way, it was still relatively simple for you to avoid graduation by switching your major periodically and obtaining a new set of special requirements. After a time, however, these began to overlap. It soon became necessary for you to switch every semester. The rule concerning mandatory graduation on completion of a departmental major was, as I understand it, passed solely because of you. You have done a lot of sidestepping, but this time you are all out of sides to step to. Time runs, the clock will strike. This is the last interview of this sort you will ever have."

"I hope so. I just came to get my card signed."

"You also asked me a question."

"Yes, but I can see now that you're busy and I'm willing to let you off the hook."

"That's quite all right. I'm here to answer your questions. To continue, when I first learned of your case, I was naturally curious as to the reason for your peculiar behavior. When I was offered the opportunity of becoming your adviser, I made it my business to find out—"

" 'Offered'? You mean you're doing this by choice?"

"Very much so. I wanted to be the one to say good-bye to you, to see you off on your way into the real world."

"If you'd just sign my card—"

"Not yet, Mister Cassidy. You wanted to know why I dislike you. When you leave here—via the door—you will know. To begin with, I have succeeded where my predecessors failed. I am familiar with the provisions of your uncle's will."

I nodded. I had had a feeling he was driving that way.

"You seem to have exceeded the scope of your appointment," I said. "That is a personal matter."

"When it touches upon your activities here, it comes within my area of interest—and speculation. As I understand it, your late uncle left a fairly sizable fund out of which you receive an extremely liberal allowance for so long as you are a full-time student working on a degree. Once you receive a degree of any sort, the allowance terminates and the balance remaining in the fund is to be distributed to representatives of the Irish Republican Army. I believe I have described the situation fairly?"

"As fairly as an unfair situation can be described, I suppose. Poor, batty old Uncle Albert. Poor me, actually. Yes, you have the facts straight."

"It would seem that the man's intention was to provide for your receiving an adequate education—no more, no less—and then leaving it to you to make your own way in the world. A most sensible notion, as I see it."

"I had already guessed that."

"And one to which you, obviously, do not subscribe."

"True. Two very different philosophies of education are obviously involved here."

"Mister Cassidy, I believe that economics rather than philosophy controls the situation. For thirteen years you have contrived to remain a full-time student without taking a degree so that your stipend would continue. You have taken gross advantage of the loophole in your uncle's will because you are a playboy and a dilettante, with no real desire ever to work, to hold a job, to repay society for suffering your existence. You are an opportunist. You are irresponsible. You are a drone."

I nodded. "All right. You have satisfied my curiosity as to your way of thinking. Thank you."

His brows fell into a frown and he studied my face.

"Since you may be my adviser for a long while," I said, "I wanted to know something of your attitude. Now I do."

He chuckled. "You are bluffing."

I shrugged. "If you'll just sign my card, I'll be on my way."

"I do not have to see that card," he said slowly, "to know that I will *not* be your adviser for a long while. This is it, Cassidy, an end to your flippancy."

I withdrew the card and extended it. He ignored it and continued. "And with your demoralizing effect here at the university, I cannot help but wonder how your uncle would feel if he knew how his wishes were being thwarted. He—"

"I'll ask him when he comes around," I said. "But when I saw him last month he wasn't exactly turning over."

"Beg pardon? I didn't quite . . ."

"Uncle Albert was one of the fortunate ones in the Bide-A-Wee scandal. About a year ago. Remember?"

He shook his head slowly. "I'm afraid not. I thought your uncle was dead. In fact, he has to be. If the will . . ."

"It's a delicate philosophical point," I said. "Legally, he's dead all right. But he had himself frozen and stored at Bide-A-Wee—one of those cryonic outfits. The proprietors proved somewhat less than scrupulous, however, and the authorities had him moved to a different establishment along with the other survivors."

"Survivors?"

"I suppose that's the best word. Bide-A-Wee had over five hundred customers on their books, but they actually only had around fifty on ice. Made a tremendous profit that way."

"I don't understand. What became of the others?"

"Their better components wound up in gray-market organ banks. That was another area where Bide- A-Wee turned a handsome profit."

"I do seem to remember hearing about it now. But what did they do with the . . . remains?"

"One of the partners also owned a funeral establishment. He just disposed of things in the course of that employment."

"Oh. Well . . . Wait a minute. What did they do if someone came around and wanted to view a frozen friend or relative?"

"They switched nameplates. One frozen body seen through a frosted panel looks pretty much like any other—sort of like a popsicle in cellophane. Anyway, Uncle Albert was one of the ones they kept for show. He always was lucky."

"How did they finally get tripped up?"

"Tax evasion. They got greedy."

"I see. Then your uncle actually could show up for an accounting one day?"

"There is always that possibility. Of course, there have been very few successful revivals."

"The possibility doesn't trouble you?"

"I deal with things as they arise. So far, Uncle Albert hasn't."

"Along with the university and your uncle's wishes, I feel obliged to point out that you are doing violence in another place as well."

I looked all around the room. Under my chair, even.

"I give up," I said.

"Yourself."

"Myself?"

"Yourself. By accepting the easy economic security of the situation, you are yielding to inertia. You are ruining your chances of ever really amounting to anything. You are growing in your dronehood."

"Dronehood?"

"Dronehood. Hanging around and not doing anything."

"So you are really acting in my best interests if you succeed in kicking me out, huh?"

"Precisely."

"I hate to tell you, but history is full of people like you. We tend to judge them harshly."

"History?"

"Not the department. The phenomenon."

He sighed and shook his head. He accepted my card, leaned back, puffed on his pipe, began to study what I had written.

I wondered whether he really believed he was doing me a favor by trying to destroy my way of life. Probably.

"Wait a minute," he said. "There's a mistake here."

"No mistake."

"The hours are wrong."

"No. I need twelve and there are twelve."

"I'm not disputing that, but—"

"Six hours, personal project, interdisciplinary, for art-history credit, on site, Australia in my case."

"You know it should really be anthropology. But that would complete a major. But that's not what I'm—"

16

"Then three hours of comparative lit with that course on the troubadours. I'm still safe with that, and I can catch it on video—the same as with that one-hour current-events thing for social-science credit. Safe there, and that's ten hours. Then two hours' credit for advanced basket weaving, and that's twelve. Home free."

"No, sir! You are not! That last one is a three-hour course, and that gives you a major in it!"

"Haven't seen Circular fifty-seven yet, have you?"

"What?"

"It's been changed."

"I don't believe you."

I glanced at his In basket.

"Read your mail."

He snatched at the basket; he rifled it. Somewhere near the middle of things he found the paper. Clocking his expressions, I noted disbelief, rage and puzzlement within the first five seconds. I was hoping for despair, but you can't have everything all at once.

Frustration and bewilderment were what remained when he turned to me once again and said, "How did you do it?"

"Why must you look for the worst?"

"Because I've read your file. You got to the instructor some way, didn't you?"

"That's most ignoble of you. And I'd be a fool to admit it, wouldn't I?"

He sighed. "I suppose so."

He withdrew a pen, clicked it with unnecessary force and scrawled his name on the "Approved by" line at the bottom of the card.

Returning the card, he observed, "This is the closest you've come, you know. It was just under the wire this time. What are you going to do for an encore?"

"I understand that two new majors will be instituted next year. I suppose I should see the proper departmental adviser if I am interested in changing my area."

"You'll see me," he said, "and I will confer with the person involved."

"Everyone else has a departmental adviser."

"You are a special case requiring special handling. You are to report here again next time."

"All right," I said, filing the card in my hip pocket as I rose. "See you then."

As I headed for the door he said, "I'll find a way."

I paused on the threshold.

"You," I said pleasantly, "and the Flying Dutchman."

I closed the door gently behind me.

2

INCIDENTS AND FRAGMENTS, bits-and-pieces time. Like—
"You're not joking?"

"I'm afraid not."

"I'd rather it looked like hell for the obvious reasons," she said, wide-eyed, backing toward the door we had just come through.

"Well, whatever happened, it's done. We'll just clean up and . . ."

She reopened the door, that long, lovely, wild hair dancing as she shook her head vigorously.

"You know, I'm going to think this over a little more," she said, stepping back into the hall.

"Aw, come on, Ginny. It's nothing serious."

"Like I said, I'll think about it."

She began closing the door.

"Should I call you later, then?"

"I don't think so."

"Tomorrow?"

"Tell you what, I'll call you."

Click.

Hell. She might as well have slammed it. End of Phase One in my search for a new roommate. Hal Sidmore, who had shared the apartment with me for some time, had gotten married a couple of months back. I missed him, as he had been a boon companion, good chess player and general heller about town, as well as an able explicator of multitudes of matters. I had decided to look for something a bit different in my next roommate, however. I thought I had spotted that indefinable quality in Ginny, late one night while climbing the radio tower behind the Pi Phi house, as she was about her end-of-day business in her third-floor room there. Things had gone swimmingly after that. I had met her at ground level, we had been doing things together for over a month and I had just about succeeded in persuading her to consider a change of residence for the coming semester. Then this.

"Damn!" I decided, kicking at a drawer that had been pulled from the desk, dumped and dropped to the floor. No sense in going after her right now. Clean up. Let her get over things. See her tomorrow.

Somebody had really torn the place apart, had gone through everything. The furniture had even been moved about and the covers pulled off the cushions. I sighed as I regarded it. Worse than the aftermath of the wildest of parties. What a rotten time for breaking and entering and breaking. It wasn't the best of neighborhoods, but it was hardly the worst. This sort of thing had never happened to me before. Now, when it did, it had to happen at precisely the wrong time, frightening away my warm and lissome companion. On top of this, something of course had to be missing.

I kept some cash and a few semivaluables in the top drawer of the bureau in my bedroom. I kept more cash tucked in the toe of an old boot on a rack in the corner. I hoped that the vandal had been satisfied with the top drawer. That was the uninspired idea behind the arrangement.

I went to see.

My bedroom was in better order than the living room, though it too had suffered some depredation. The bed clothing had been pulled off and the mattress was askew. Two of the bureau drawers were open but undumped. I crossed the room, opened the top drawer and looked inside.

Everything was still in place, even the money. I moved to the rack, checked my boot. The roll of bills was still where I had left it.

"There's a good fellow. Now toss it here" came a familiar voice that I could not quite place in that context.

Turning, I saw that Paul Byler, Professor of Geology, had just emerged from my closet. His hands were empty, not that he needed a weapon to back up any threat. While short, he was powerfully built, and I had always been impressed by the quantity of scar tissue on those knuckles. An Australian, he had started out as a mining engineer in some pretty raw places, only later picking up his graduate work in geology and physics and getting into teaching.

But I had always been on excellent terms with the man, even after I had departed my geology major. I had known him socially for several years. Hadn't seen him for the past couple of weeks, though, as he had taken some leave. I had thought he was out of town.

So: "Paul, what's the matter?" I said. "Don't tell me you did all this messing?"

"The boot, Fred. Just pass me the boot."

"If you're short on cash, I'll be glad to lend you—"

"The boot!"

I took it to him. I stood there and watched as he plunged his hand inside, felt about, withdrew my roll of bills. He snorted then and thrust the boot and the money back at me, hard. I dropped both, because he had caught me in the abdomen.

Before I even completed a brief curse, he had seized me by the shoulders, spun me about and shoved me into the armchair beside the open window where the curtains fluttered lightly in the breeze.

"I don't want your money, Fred," he said, glaring at me. "I just want something you have that belongs to me. Now you had better give me an honest answer. Do you know what I'm talking about or don't you?"

"I haven't the foggiest," I said. "I don't have anything of yours. You could have just called me and asked me that. You didn't have to come busting in here and—"

He slapped me. Not especially hard. Just enough to jolt me and leave me silent.

"Fred," he said, "shut up. Just shut up and listen. Answer when I ask you a question. That's all. Keep the comments for another day. I'm in a hurry. Now I know you are lying because I've already seen your ex-roommate Hal. He says you have it, because he left it here when he moved out. What I am referring to is one of my models of the star-stone, which he picked up after a poker party in my lab. Remember?"

"Yes," I said. "If you had just called me and ask—"

He slapped me again. "Where is it?"

I shook my head, partly to clear it and partly in negation.

"I . . . I don't know," I said.

He raised his hand.

"Wait! I'll explain! He had that thing you gave him out on the desk, in the front room, was using it for a paperweight. I'm sure he took it with him—along with all his other stuff—when he moved out. I haven't seen it for a couple of months. I'm sure of that."

"Well, one of you is lying," he said, "and you're the one I've got."

He swung again, but this time I was ready for him. I ducked and kicked him in the groin.

It was spectacular. Almost worth staying to watch, as I had never kicked anyone in the groin before. The cold, rational thing to do next would be to go for the back of his neck while he was doubled over that way, preferably spiking him with my elbow. However, I was not in a cold, rational mood just then. To be honest about it, I was afraid of the man, scared to get too close to him. Having had small experience with groin-kicked persons, I had no idea how long it might be before he straightened up and came at me.

Which is why I took to my own element rather than stay there and face him.

I was over the arm of the chair, had the window the rest of the way up and was out it in an instant. There was a narrow ledge along which I moved until I had hold of the drainpipe, off about eight feet to the right.

I could continue on around it, go up or down. But I decided to remain where I was. I felt secure.

Not too much later his head emerged from the window, turned my way. He studied the ledge and cursed me. I lit a cigarette and smiled.

"What are you waiting for?" I said when he paused for breath. "Come on out. You may be a lot tougher than I am, Paul, but if you come out here only one of us is going back in again. That's concrete down there. Come on. Talk is cheap. Show me."

He took a deep breath and his grip tightened on the sill. For a moment I actually thought he was going to try it. He looked downward, though, and he looked back at me.

"All right, Fred," he said, getting control of his lecture voice. "I'm not that big a fool. You win. But listen, please. What I've said is true. I've got to have that thing back. I would not have acted as I did if it were not very important. Please tell me, if you will, whether you were telling me the truth."

I was still smarting from those slaps. I did not feel like being a nice guy. On the other hand, it must have meant a lot to him to make him behave as he had, and I had nothing to gain by not telling him. So: "It was the truth," I said.

"And you have no idea where it might be?"

"None."

"Could someone have picked it up?"

"Easily."

"Who?"

"Anybody. You know those parties we had. Thirty, forty people in there."

He nodded and gnashed his teeth.

"All right," he said then. "I believe you. Try and think, though. Can you recall anything—anything at all—that might give me a lead?"

I shook my head. "Sorry."

He sighed. He sagged. He looked away.

"Okay," he said finally. "I'm going now. I suppose you plan on calling the police?"

"Yes."

"Well, I'm in no position to ask favors, or to threaten you, at the moment. But this is both—a request and a warning of whatever future reprisal I might be able to manage. Don't call them. I've troubles enough without having to worry about them, too."

He turned away.

"Wait," I said.

"What?"

"Maybe if you tell me what the problem is . . ."

"No. You can't help me."

"Well, supposing the thing turned up? What should I do with it?"

"If that should happen, put it in a safe place and keep your mouth shut about having it. I'll call you periodically. Tell me about it then."

"What's so important about it?"

"Un-uh," he said, and was gone.

A whispered question from behind me—"Do you see me, red?"—and I turned, but there was no one there, though my ears still rang from the boxing they had taken. I decided then that it was a bad day and I took to the roof for some thinking. A traffic-copter buzzed me later, and I was queried as to suicidal intentions. I told the cop I was refribbing shingles, though, and that seemed to satisfy him.

Incidents and fragments continued—

"I *did* try phoning you. Three times," he said. "No answer."

"Did you consider stopping by in person?"

"I was about to. Just now. You got here first."

"Did you call the police?"

"No. I've got a wife to worry about as well as myself."

"I see."

"Did you call them?"

"No."

"Why not?"

"I'm not certain. Well, I guess it's that I'd like a better idea as to what's going on before I blow the whistle on him."

Hal nodded, a dark-eyed study in bruise and Bandaid.

"And you think I know something you don't?"

"That's right."

"Well, I don't," he said, taking a sip, wincing and stirring more sugar into his iced tea. "When I answered the door earlier, there he was. I let him in and he started asking me about that damned stone. I told him everything I could remember, but he still wasn't satisfied. That was when he began pushing me around."

"Then what happened?"

"I remembered some more things."

"Uh-huh. Like you remembered I have it—which I don't— so he'd come rough me up and leave you alone."

"No! That's not it at all!" he said. "I told him the truth. I left it there when I moved out. As to what became of it afterwards, I have no idea."

"Where'd you leave it?"

"Last I remember seeing it, it was on the desk."

"Why didn't you take it with you?"

"I don't know. I was tired of looking at it, I guess."

He got up and paced his living room, paused and looked out the window. Mary was off attending a class, a thing she had also been doing that afternoon when Paul had stopped by, had his conference with Hal and started the ball rolling down the alley that led to me.

"Hal," I said, "are you telling me the whole truth and nothing but?"

"Everything important."

"Come on."

He turned his back to the window, looked at me, looked away.

"Well," he said, "he claimed the thing we had was his."

I ignored the "we."

"It was," I said, "once. But I was there when he gave it to you. Title passed."

But Hal shook his head. "Not that simple," he said.

"Oh?"

He returned to sit with his iced tea. He drummed his fingers on the tabletop, took a quick sip, looked at me again.

"No," he said. "You see, the one we had was really his. Remember that night we got it? We played cards in his lab till pretty late. The six stones were on a shelf above the counter. We noticed them early and asked him about them several times. He would just smile and say something mysterious or change the subject. Then, as the night wore on and after he'd had more to drink, he began talking about them, told us what they were."

"I remember," I said. "He told us he had been to see the star-stone, which had just that week been received from the aliens and put on display in New York. He had taken hundreds of photographs through all sorts of filters, filled a notebook with observations, collected all the data he could. Then he had set out to construct a model of the thing. Said he was going to find a way to produce them cheaply, to sell them as novelty items. The half dozen on his shelf represented his best efforts at that point. He thought they were pretty good."

"Right. Then I noticed that there were several rejects in the waste bin beside the counter. I picked out the best-looking one and held it up to the light. It was a pretty thing, just like the others. Paul smiled when he saw that I had it, and he said, 'You like it?' I told him that I did. 'Keep it,' he said."

"So you did. That's the way I remember it, too."

"Yes, but there was more to it than that," he said. "I took it back to the table with me and set it down next to my money—so that each time I reached over for some change, I automatically glanced at it. After a time I became aware of a tiny flaw, a little imperfection at the base of one of the limbs. It was quite insignificant, but it irritated me more and more each time that I looked at it. So, when you two left the room later, to bring in more cold beer and sodas, I took it over and switched it with one of those on the shelf."

"I begin to see."

"Okay, okay! I probably shouldn't have done it. I didn't see any harm in it at the time. They were just prototype souvenirs he was fooling with, and the difference wasn't even noticeable unless you were looking hard."

"He'd noticed it the first time around."

"Which was good reason for him to consider them perfect and not be looking again. And what difference did it make, really? Even in the absence of a six-pack the answer seems obvious."

"It sounds all right, I'll give you that. But the fact is that he *did* check—and it also seems that they were more important than he had indicated. I wonder why?"

"I've been doing a lot of thinking," he said. "The first thing that occurred to me was that the souvenir business was just a story he made up because he wanted to show them off to us and he had to tell us something. Supposing he had been approached by someone from the UN to produce a model— several models—for them? The original is priceless, irreplaceable and on display to the public. To guard against theft or someone with a compulsion and a sledgehammer, it would seem wisest to keep it locked away and put a phony one in the showcase. Paul would be a logical choice for the job. Whenever anyone talks crystallography, his name comes up."

"I could buy parts of that," I said, "but the whole thing doesn't hang together. Why get so upset over the flawed specimen when he could just manufacture another? Why not simply write off the one we've lost?"

"Security?"

"If that's so, we didn't break it. He did. Why shove us around and bring it to mind when we were doing a good job forgetting about it? No, that doesn't seem to jibe."

"All right, what then?"

I shrugged.

"Insufficient data," I said, getting to my feet. "If you decide to call the police, be sure to tell them that the thing he was looking for was something you'd stolen from him."

"Aw, Fred, that's hitting below the belt."

"It's true, though. I wonder what the intrinsic value of the thing was? I forget where they draw the misdemeanor-felony line."

"Okay, you've made your point. What are you going to do?"

I shrugged. "Nothing, I guess. Wait and see what happens, I suppose. Let me know if you think of anything else."

28

"All right. You do the same?"

"Yes."

I started toward the door.

"Sure you won't stay for dinner?" he said.

"No, thanks. I've got to run."

"See you, then."

"Right. Take it easy."

Walking past a darkened bakery. Play of night and light on glass. DO YOU TASTE ME BRED? I read. I hesitated, turned, saw where shadows had anagrammatized a bake sale, sniffed, hurried on.

Bits and pieces—

Near midnight, as I was trying a new route up the cathedral, I thought that I counted an extra gargoyle. As I moved closer, though, I saw that it was Professor Dobson atop the buttress. Drunk again and counting stars, I guessed.

I continued, coming to rest on a nearby ledge.

"Good evening, Professor."

"Hello, Fred. Yes, it is, isn't it? Beautiful night. I was hoping you'd pass this way. Have a drink."

"Low tolerance," I said. "I seldom indulge."

"Special occasion," he suggested.

"Well, a little then."

I accepted the bottle he extended, took a sip.

"Good. Very good," I said, passing it back. "What is it? And what's the occasion?"

"A very, very special cognac I've been saving for over twenty years, for tonight. The stars have finally run their fiery routes to the proper places, positioned with elegant cunning, possessed of noble portent."

"What do you mean?"

"I'm retiring, getting out of this lousy rat race."

"Oh, congratulations. I hadn't heard."

"That was by design. Mine. I can't stand formal good-byes. Just a few more loose ends to splice, and I'll be ready to go. Next week probably."

"Well, I hope you have an enjoyable time of it. It is not often that I meet someone with the interest we share. I'll miss you."

He took a sip from his bottle, nodded, grew silent. I lit a cigarette, looked out across the sleeping town, up at the stars. The night was cool, the breeze more than a little damp. Small traffic sounds came and went, distant, insectlike. An occasional bat interrupted my tracing of constellations.

"Alkaid, Mizar, Alioth," I murmured, "Megrez, Phecda . . ."

"Merak and Dubhe," he said, finishing off the Big Dipper and surprising me, both for having overheard and for knowing the rest.

"Back where I left them so many years ago," he went on. "I've a very peculiar feeling now—the thing I set out to analyze tonight. Did you ever look back at some moment in your past and have it suddenly grow so vivid that all the intervening years seemed brief, dreamlike, impersonal—the motions of a May afternoon surrendered to routine?"

"No," I said.

"One day, when you do, remember—the cognac," he said, and he took another sip and passed me the bottle.

I had some more and returned it to him.

"They did actually creep, though, those thousands of days. Petty pace, and all that," he continued. "I know this intellectually, though something else is currently denying it. I am aware of it particularly, because I am especially conscious of the difference between that earlier time and this present. It was a cumulative thing, the change. Space travel, cities under the sea, the advances in medicine—even our first contact with the aliens—all of these things occurred at different times and everything else seemed unchanged when they did. Petty pace. Life pretty

30

much the same but for this one new thing. Then another, at another time. Then another. No massive revolution. An incremental process is what it was. Then suddenly a man is ready to retire, and this gives rise to reflection. He looks back, back to Cambridge, where a young man is climbing a building. He sees those stars. He feels the texture of that roof. Everything that follows is a blur, a kaleidoscopic monochrome. He is here and he is there. Everything else is unreal. But they are two different worlds, Fred—two completely different worlds—and he didn't really see it happen, never actually caught either one in the act of going or coming. And that is the feeling that accompanies me tonight."

"Is it a good feeling or a bad one?" I said.

"I don't really know. I haven't worked up an emotion to go with it yet."

"Let me know when you do, will you? You've got me curious."

He chuckled. I did, too.

"You know, it's funny," I said, "that you never stopped climbing."

He was silent for a while, then said, "About the climbing, it's rather peculiar . . . Of course, it was somewhat in the nature of a tradition where I was a student, though I believe I liked it more than most. I kept at it for several years after I left the university, and then it became a more or less sporadic thing with changes of residence and lack of opportunity. I would get spells, though—compulsions, actually—when I just had to climb. I would take a holiday, then, to someplace where the architecture was congenial. I'd spend my nights scaling the buildings, clambering about rooftops and spires."

"Acrophilia," I said.

"True. Baptizing a thing doesn't explain it, though. I never understood why I did it. Still don't, for that matter. I did finally stop it for a long while, though. Middle-age hormone shift perhaps. Who knows? Then I came here to teach. It was when I heard of your own activities that I began thinking about it again. This led to the desire, the act, the return of the compulsion. It has been with me ever since. I've spent mare time wondering why people quit climbing things than why they start."

"It does seem the natural thing to do."

"Exactly."

He took another drink, offered me one. I would have liked to but I know my limits, and sitting there on the ledge, I was not about to push them. So he gestured with the bottle, skyward, then: "To the lady with the smile," he said, and drank it for me.

"To the rocks of empire," he added a moment later, with a swing and a swig to another starry sector. The wrong one, but no matter. He knew as well as I that it was still below the horizon.

He settled back, found a cigar, lit it, mused: "How many eyes per head, I wonder, in the place they regard the 'Mona Lisa'? Are they faceted? Fixed? And of what color?"

"Only two. You know that. And sort of hazel—in the pictures, anyway."

"Must you deflate romantic rhetoric? Besides, the Astabigans have plenty of visitors from other worlds who will be viewing her."

"True. And for that matter, the British Crown Jewels are in the custody of people with crescent-shaped pupils. Kind of lavender-eyed, I believe."

"Sufficient," he said. "Redeeming. Thank you."

A shooting star burned its way earthward. My cigarette butt followed it.

"I wonder if it was a fair trade?" he said. "We don't understand the Rhennius machine, and even the aliens aren't certain what the star-stone represents."

"It wasn't exactly a trade."

"Two of the treasures of Earth are gone and we have a couple of theirs in return. What else would you call it?"

"A link in a *kula* chain," I said.

"I am not familiar with the term. Tell me about it."

"The parallel struck me as I read the details of the deal we had been offered. The *kula* is a kind of ceremonial voyage undertaken at various times by the inhabitants of the island groups to the east of New Guinea—the Trobriand Islanders, the Papuans of Melanesia. It is a sort of double circuit, a movement in two opposite directions among the islands. The purpose is the mutual exchange of articles having no special functional value to the various tribes involved, but possessed of great cultural significance. Generally, they are body ornaments—necklaces, bracelets—bearing names and colorful histories. They move slowly about the great circuit of the islands, accompanied by their ever-growing histories, are exchanged with considerable pomp and ceremony and serve to focus cultural enthusiasm in a way that promotes a certain unity, a sense of mutual obligation and trust. Now, the general similarity to the exchange program we are entering with the aliens seems pretty obvious. The objects become both cultural hostages and emblems of honor to the trustees. By their existence, their circulation, their display, they inevitably create something of a community feeling. This is the true purpose of a *kula* chain, as I see it. That's why I didn't like the word 'trade.' "

"Most interesting. None of the reports I've heard or read put it in that light—and certainly none of them compared it to the *kula* phenomenon. They cast it more in terms of an initiation fee for joining the galactic club, the price of admission to enjoy the benefits of trade and the exchange of ideas. That sort of thing."

"That was just the sales pitch, to ease public protest over the relinquishment of cultural treasures. All we were really promised was reciprocity in the chain. I'm sure those other things will eventually come to pass, but not necessarily as a direct result. No. Our governments were indulging in the time-honored practice of giving the people a simple, palatable explanation of a complex thing."

"I can see that," he said, and he stretched and yawned. "In fact, I prefer your interpretation over the official one."

I lit another cigarette.

"Thanks," I said. "I feel obligated to point out, though, that I have always been a sucker for ideas I find aesthetically pleasing. The cosmic sweep of the thing—an interstellar *kula* chain—affirming the differences and at the same time emphasizing the similarities of all the intelligent races in the galaxy—tying them together, building common traditions . . . The notion strikes me as kind of fine."

"Obviously," he said, gesturing then toward the higher stages of the cathedral. "Tell me, are you going to climb the rest of the way up tonight?"

"Probably, in a little while. Did you want to go now?"

"No, no. I was just curious. You generally go all the way to the top, don't you?"

"Yes. Don't you?"

"Not always. In fact, I've recently been keeping more to the middle heights. The reason I asked, though, is that I have a question, seeing that you are in a philosophical mood."

"It's catching."

"All right. Then tell me what it feels like when you reach the top."

"An elation, I guess. A sense of accomplishment, sort of."

"Up here the view is less obstructed. You can see farther, take in more of the features of the landscape. Is that it, I wonder? A better perspective?"

"Part of it, maybe. But there is always one other thing I feel when I reach the top: I always want to go just a little bit higher, and I always feel that I almost can, that I am just about to."

"Yes. That's true," he said.

"Why do you ask?"

"I don't know. To be reminded, perhaps. That boy in Cambridge would have said the same thing you did, but I had partly forgotten. It is not just the world that has changed."

He took another drink.

"I wonder," he said, "what it was really like? That first encounter—out there—with the aliens. Hard to believe that several years have passed since it happened. The governments obviously glossed up the story, so we will probably never know exactly what was said or done. A coincidental run-in, neither of us familiar with the system where we met. Exploring, that's all. It was doubtless less of a shock to them, being acquainted with so many other races across the galaxy. Still . . . I remember that unexpected return. Mission accomplished. A half century ahead of schedule. Accompanied by an Astabigan scouting vessel. If an object attains the speed of light it turns into a pumpkin. Everybody knew that. But the aliens had found a way of cheating space out of its pumpkins, and they brought our ship back through the tunnel they made under it. Or across the bridge over it. Or something like that. Lots of business for the math department. Strange feeling. Not at all the way I had thought it might be. Sort of like working your way up a steeple or a dome—really difficult going—and then, when you reach the point where you realize you've got it made, you look up and see that someone else is already there on top. So we'd run into a galactic civilization—a loose confederation of races that's been in existence for millennia. Maybe we were lucky. It could easily have taken a couple more centuries. Maybe not, though.

My feelings were, and still are, mixed. How can you go a little bit higher after something that anticlimactic? They've given us the technical know-how to build pumpkin-proof ships of our own. They've also warned us off a lot of celestial real estate. They've granted us a place in their exchange program, where we're bound to make a poor showing. Changes will be coming faster and faster in the years ahead. The world may even begin to change at a noticeable rate. What then? Once that petty-pace quality is lost, everyone may wind up as bewildered as a drunken old nightclimber on a cathedral who has been vouchsafed a glimpse of the clicking gear teeth between himself here and the towers of Cambridge there, wherever. What then? See the mainspring and turn to pumpkins? Retire? Alkaid, Mizar, Alioth, Megrez, Phecda, Merak and Dubhe . . . *They* have been there. *They* know them. Perhaps, deep down inside, I wanted us to be alone in the cosmos—to claim all of that for ourselves. Or any aliens encountered, a little behind us in everything. Greedy, proud, selfish . . . True. Now, though, we're the provincials, God help us! Enough left to drink to our health. Good! Here's to it! I spit into the face of Time that has transfigured me!"

Offhand, I could think of nothing to say, so I said nothing. Part of me wanted to agree with him, but only part. For that matter, part of me sort of wished he had not finished off the brandy.

After a time he said, "I don't think I'll be doing any more climbing tonight," and I reckoned that a good idea. I had decided against further altitude myself, and, wheeling, we narrowed our gyre, down and around and down, and I saw the good man home.

Bits and pieces. Pieces—

I caught the tag end of the late late news before turning in. A fog-dispelling item involved a Paul Byler, Professor of Geology, set upon by vandals in Central Park earlier that evening, who, in addition to whatever money he was carrying, had been deprived by the rascals of heart, liver, kidneys and lungs.

Some upwelling in the dark fishbowl atop the spine later splashed dreams, patterns memory-resistant as a swirl of noctilucae, across consciousness' thin, transparent rim, save for the kinesthetic/synthetic DO YOU FEEL ME LED? which must have lasted a timeless time longer than the rest, for later, much later, morning's third coffee touched it to a penny's worth of spin, of color.

3

SUNFLASH, SOME SPLASH. Darkle. Stardance.

Phaeton's solid gold Cadillac crashed where there was no ear to hear, lay burning, flickered, went out. Like me.

At least, when I woke again it was night and I was a wreck.

Lying there, bound with rawhide straps, spread-eagle, sand and gravel for pillow as well as mattress, dust in my mouth, nose, ears and eyes, dined upon by vermin, thirsty, bruised, hungry and shaking, I reflected on the words of my onetime adviser, Doctor Merimee: "You are a living example of the absurdity of things."

Needless to say, his specialty was the novel, French, mid-twentieth century Yet, yet do those lens-distorted eyes touch like spikes the extremities of my condition. Despite his departure from the university long ago under the cloud of a scandal involving a girl, a dwarf and a donkey—or perhaps because of this—Merimee has, over the years, come to occupy something of an oracular position in my private cosmos, and his words often return to me in contexts other than that of the preregistration interview. The hot sands had shouted them through me all afternoon, then night's frigid breezes had whispered the motto at the overdone lamb chop, my ear: "You are a living example of the absurdity of things."

Open to a variety of interpretations when you stop to think about it, and I had plenty of time to, just then. On the one hand, it could put me on the side of the things. On the other, the living. Or, perhaps, on the other, the absurdity.

Oh yes. Hands . . .

I tried flexing my fingers, wasn't sure they obeyed. Could be they weren't really there and I was feeling a faint phantom limb effect. Just in case they still were, I thought about gangrene for a while.

Damn. And again. Frustrating, this.

The semester had opened and I had departed. After making arrangements to mail my advanced baskets to my audible partner Ralph at the crafts shop, I had headed west, tarrying equally in San Francisco, Honolulu, Tokyo. A pair of peaceful weeks had passed. Then a brief stay in Sydney. Just long enough to get into trouble climbing around that fishswallowing-fish-swallowing-fish opera house they have out on Bennelong Point overlooking the harbor. I left town with a limp and a reprimand. Flew to Alice Springs. Picked up the air scooter I had ordered. Took off in the early morning before the full heat of day and light of reason made their respective ways into the world. The countryside struck me as a good place to send trainee saints to get what was coming to them. It took several hours to locate the site and a few more to dig in and set things up. I did not anticipate a long stay.

There are carvings on the cliff walls, quite old, covering around 1,600 square feet. The aborigines in the area disclaim any knowledge of their origin or purpose. I had seen photographs, but I had wanted to view the real thing, try some shots of my own, take rubbings and do a little digging around.

I got into the shade of my shelter, sipped sodas and tried to think cool thoughts as I regarded the work on the rock. While I seldom indulge in graffiti, verbal or pre-, I have always felt something of empathy for those who scale walls and make their marks on them. The farther back you go, the more interesting the act becomes. Now it may be true, as some have claimed, that the impulse was first felt in the troglodytic equivalent of the john and that cave drawings got started this way, as a kind of pictorial sublimation of an even more primitive evolutionary means of marking one's territory. Nevertheless, when somebody started climbing around on walls and mountainsides to do it, it seems pretty obvious that it had grown from a pastime into an art form. I have often thought of that first guy with a mastodon in his head, staring at a cliff face or cave wall, and I have wondered what it was that set him suddenly to climbing and scraping away—what it felt like. Also, what the public's reaction was. Perhaps they made sufficient holes in him to insure the egress of the spirits behind it all. Or perhaps the bold initiative involved was present in greater abundance then, awaiting only the proper stimulus, and a bizarre response was considered as common as the wriggling of one's ears. Impossible to say. Difficult not to care.

Whatever, I took photographs that afternoon, dug holes that evening and the following morning. Spent most of the second day taking rubbings and more photos. Continued my base trench at daysend, coming across what seemed the pieces of a blunted stone chisel. Nothing quite that interesting turned up the next morning, though I kept at the digging long past the hour I had marked for quitting.

I retired to the shade then to nurse blisters and restore my balance of liquids while I wrote up the day's doings to that point along with some fresh thoughts that had occurred to me concerning the entire enterprise. I broke for lunch around one o'clock and doodled in my notebook again for a time afterward.

It was a little after three when a skycar passed overhead, then turned back, descending. This troubled me a bit, as I had absolutely no official authorization for what I was doing. On some piece of paper, card, tape, or all of these, somewhere, I was listed as "tourist." I had no idea whether a permit was required for what I was about, though I strongly suspected this. Time means a lot to me, paperwork wastes it, and I have always been a firm believer in my right to do anything I cannot be stopped from doing. Which sometimes entails not getting caught at it. This is not quite so bad as it sounds, as I am a decent, civilized, likable guy. So, shading my eyes against the blue and fiery afternoon, I began searching for ways to convince the authorities of this. Lying, I decided, was probably best.

It came to earth and two men alit. Their appearance was not what I would ordinarily consider official, but allowance for custom and circumstance is always in order and I rose to meet them. The first man was around my height—that is, a little under six feet—but heavily built and beginning work on a paunch. His hair and eyes were light, he had a mild sunburn and was slick with sweat. His companion was a couple of inches taller, a couple of shades darker and brushed an unruly strand of dark brown hair back from his forehead as he advanced. He was lean and fit-looking. Both wore city shoes rather than boots, and their lack of head protection in that heat struck me as peculiar.

"You Fred Cassidy?" said the first man, coming to within a few paces of me and turning away to regard the wall and my trench.

"Yes," I said, "I am."

He produced a surprisingly delicate handkerchief and patted his face with it.

"Find what you were looking for?" he asked.

"Wasn't looking for anything special," I said.

He chuckled. "Seems as if you did an awful lot of work, looking for nothing."

"That's just an exploratory trench," I said.

"Why are you exploring?"

"How about telling me who you are and why you want to know?" I said.

He ignored my question and went over to the trench. He paced along its length, stooping a couple of times and peering down into it. While he was doing this, the other man walked over to my shelter. I called out as he reached for my knapsack, but he opened it and dumped it anyway.

He was into my shaving kit by the time I got to him. I took hold of his arm, but he jerked it away. When I tried again, he pushed me back and I stumbled. Before I hit the ground, I had decided that they were not cops.

Rather than getting up for the next performance, I kicked out from where I lay and raked him across the shins with the heel of my boot. It was not quite as spectacular as the time I had kicked Paul Byler in the groin but was more than sufficient for my purposes. I scrambled to my feet then and caught him on the chin with a hard left. He collapsed and did not move. Not bad for one punch. If I could do it without a rock in my hand I'd be a holy terror.

My triumph lasted all of a pair of seconds. Then a sack of cannonballs was dropped on my back, or so it seemed. I was clipped from behind and borne to the ground in a very un-sportsmanlike fashion. The heavyset one was much faster than his appearance had led me to believe, and as he twisted my arm up behind my back and caught hold of my hair I began to real-ize that little, if any, of his bulk was of the non-functional, fatty variety. Even that central bulge was a curbstone.

"All right, Fred. I guess it's time to have our talk," he said.

Stardance . . .

Lying there, with my abrasions, contusions, aches and con-fusions, I decided that Professor Merimee had come very near that still, cold center of things where definition lurks. Absurd indeed was the manner in which a dead hand was extended to give me the finger.

Lying there, cursing subvocally as I retraced my route to the moment, I became peripherally aware of a small, dark, furry form moving along my southern boundary, pausing, staring, moving again. Doubtless something carnivorous, I decided. I fought with a shudder, transformed it into a shrug. There was no point in calling out. None whatsoever. But there could be a small measure of triumph to going out this way.

So I tried to cultivate stoicism while straining after a better view of the beast. It touched my right leg and I jerked convulsively, but there was no pain. After a time, it moved over to my left. Had it just eaten my numbed foot? I wondered. Had it enjoyed it?

Moments later it turned again, advancing upward along my left side, and I finally got a better look at it. I saw a stupid-looking little marsupial that I recognized as a wombat, harmless-seeming and apparently curious, hardly lusting after my extremities. I sighed and felt some of the tension go out of me. It was welcome to sniff around all it cared to. When you are going to die, a wombat is better than no company at all.

I thought back to the weight and the twisting of my arm, as the heavy man, ignoring his fallen companion, had sat upon me and said, "All that I really want of you is the stone. Where is it?"

"Stone?" I had said, making the mistake of adding the question mark.

The pressure on my arm increased.

"Byler's stone," he said. "You know the one I mean."

"Yes, I do!" I agreed. "Let up, will you? It's no secret what happened. I'll tell you all about it."

"Go ahead," he said, easing up a fraction.

So I told him about the facsimile and how we had come by it. I told him everything I knew about the damned thing.

As I feared, he did not believe a word I said. Worse yet, his partner recovered while I was talking. He was also of the opinion that I was lying, and he voted to continue the questioning.

This was done, and at one point many red and electric minutes later, as they paused to massage their knuckles and catch their breath, the tall one said to the heavy one, "Sounds pretty much like what he told Byler."

"Like what Byler *said* he told him," the other corrected.

"If you talked to Paul," I said, "what more can I tell you? He seemed to know what was going on—which I don't—and I told him everything I knew about the stone: exactly what I've just told you."

"Oh, we talked to him, all right," the tall man said, "and he talked to us. You might say he spilled his guts—"

"But I wasn't sure of him then," the fat man said, "and I'm less sure of him now. What do you do the minute he kicks off? You head for his old stamping grounds and start digging holes. I think the two of you were in this together somehow and that you had matching stories worked out in advance. I think the stone is around here someplace, and I think you have a pretty good idea how to put your hands on it. So you will tell us. You can do it the easy way or the hard way. Make your choice."

"I've already told you—"

"You've made your choice," he said.

The period that followed proved something less than satisfactory for all parties concerned. They obtained nothing that they wanted, and so did I. My greatest fear at the time was mutilation. From a pummeling I can recover. If someone is willing to lop off fingers or poke out an eye, though, it puts talking or not talking a lot closer to a life-death situation. But once you start that business, it is a kind of irreversible thing.

44

The interrogator has to keep going himself one better for so long as there is resistance, and eventually there is a point where death becomes preferable to life for the subject. Once that point is achieved, it becomes something of a race between the two of them, with information as one goal and death the other. Of course, uncertainty as to whether the interrogator may go this far can be just about as effective as knowing that he will. In this case, I was pretty certain they were capable of it, because of Byler. But the heavy man was unhappy with Paul's story, I could see that. If I were to reach that same turning point and then win the race, he would be even less happy. Since he was unwilling to believe that I really did not have the information he was after, he must have assumed that I had fortitude to spare. I guess this determined his decision to proceed carefully, while in no way reducing the harsher eventuality.

All of which I offer as preamble to his comment, "Let's put him in the sun and watch him turn into a raisin," followed by several moments of silken brow-blotting as he awaited my response. Disappointed by it, they staked me out where I could wrinkle, darken and concentrate my sugars, while they returned to their vehicle for an ice chest. They took up a position in the shade of my shelter, periodically strolling over to stage a beer commercial on my behalf.

Thus the afternoon. Later, they decided that a night's worth of wind, sand and stars were also necessary for my raisinhood. So they fetched sleeping bags and the makings of a meal from their vehicle and proceeded to encamp. If they thought the cooking odors would make me hungry, they were wrong. They just made me sick to my stomach.

I watched the day drive west. The man in the moon was standing on his head.

How long I had been unconscious I did not know. There were no sounds of movement from the camp and I could see no light in that direction. The wombat had crawled off to my right and settled there, making soft, rhythmic noises. He rested partly against my arm and I could feel his movements, his breathing.

I still did not know my tormentors' names, nor had I obtained a single new fact concerning the object of their inquiries, the star-stone. Not that it should actually have mattered, save in an academic sense. Not at that point. I was certain that I was going to die before very long. The night had delivered a jaw-jittering chill, and if it didn't finish me I figured my inquisitors would.

My recollection from a physiological psychology course was that it is not the absolute state of a sense organ that we perceive but rather its rate of change. Thus, if I could keep quite still, could emulate the Japanese in a steaming bath, the cold sensations should drop. But this was a matter of comfort rather than one of survival. While relief was my immediate objective, I spotted the notion of continued existence lurking at the back of my thoughts. I did not take a stick to it, however, because its methods seemed useful—which of course seems another way of saying that I am weak and irresolute. I won't argue.

There is a rhythmic breathing technique that always made me feel warmer when I practiced it in my yoga class. I commenced the exercise, but my breath escaped me in a rattling wheeze. I choked and began to cough.

The wombat turned and sprang onto my chest. I began to scream, but he stuffed his paw into my mouth, gagging me. With my left hand I reached for the scruff of his neck and had hold of it before I recalled that my left hand was supposedly bound.

He clamped down with his other three limbs, thrust his face up close to mine and whispered hoarsely, "You are complicating

46

matters dangerously, Mister Cassidy. Release my neck immediately and keep still afterwards."

Obviously, then, I was delirious. Comfort within the framework of my delirium seemed a desirable end, however, so I let go his neck and attempted to nod. He withdrew his paw.

"Very good," he said. "Your feet are already free. I just have to finish undoing your right hand and we will be ready to go."

"Go?" I said.

"Shsh!" he said, moving off to the right once more.

So I shshed while he worked on the strap. It was the most interesting hallucination I had had in a long while. I sought among my various neuroses after the reason for its taking this form. Nothing suggested itself immediately. But then neuroses are tricky little devils, according to Doctor Marko, and one must give them their due when it comes to subtlety and sneakiness.

"There!" he whispered moments later. "You are free. Follow me!"

He began to move away.

"Wait!"

He paused, turned back.

"What is the matter?" he asked.

"I can't move yet. Give my circulation a chance, will you? My hands and feet are numb."

He snorted and returned.

"Then movement is the best therapy," he said, seizing my arm and drawing me forward into a sitting position.

He was amazingly strong for a hallucination, and he continued dragging on my arm until I fell forward onto all fours. I was shaky, but I held the pose.

"Good," he said, patting my shoulder. "Come on."

"Wait! I'm dying of thirst."

"Sorry. I am traveling light. If you will follow me, however, I can promise you a drink."

"When?"

"Never," he snarled, "if you just sit there. In fact, I think I hear some noises back at the camp now. Come on!"

I began crawling toward him. He said, "Keep low," which was rather unnecessary, as I was unable to get to my feet. He moved away from the camp then, heading in a generally easterly direction, roughly parallel to the ridge beside which I had been working. My progress was slow, and he paused periodically to allow me to catch up.

I followed for several minutes, and then a throbbing began in my extremities, accompanied by flashes of feeling. This collapsed me, and I croaked some obscenity as I fell. He bounded toward me, but I bit off my outburst before he could repeat the paw-in-mouth trick.

"You are a very difficult creature to rescue," he stated. "Along with your circulatory system, your judgment and self-control seem to be of a primitive order."

I found another obscenity, but I whispered this one.

"Which you continue to demonstrate," he added. "You need do only two things—follow and keep silent. You are not very good at either. It causes one to wonder—"

"Get moving!" I said. "I'll follow!"

"And your emotions—"

I lunged at him, but he darted back and away.

I followed, ignoring everything but the desire to throttle the little beast. It did not matter that the situation was patently absurd. I had both Merimee and Marko to draw upon for theory, an opposing pair of fun-house mirrors with me in the middle, hot on the trail of the wombat. I followed, muttering, burning adrenalin, spitting out the dust he raised. I lost track of time.

The ridge grew lower, broke up. We moved inward, upward, then downward, passing through rocky corridors into a deeper darkness, moving over a way that was now all stone and gravel. I slipped once, and he was beside me in an instant.

"Are you all right?" he asked.

I started to laugh, controlled it.

"Sure, I'm fine."

He was careful to stay out of reach.

"It is just a little farther," he said. "Then you can rest. I will fetch you nourishment."

"I am sorry," I said, struggling to rise and failing, "but this is it. If I can wait up ahead, I can wait here. I'm out of gas."

"The way *is* rocky," he said, "and they should not be able to track you. But I would feel better if you could continue just a little farther. There is an alcove off to the side, you see. If you were in there, chances are they would pass without seeing you if they should happen to stumble on this trail. What do you say?"

"I say it sounds good, but I don't think I can do it."

"Try again. One more time."

"All right."

I pushed myself up, wobbled, advanced. If I fell again, that was it, I decided. I would have to take my chances. I was feeling lightheaded as well as heavybodied.

But I persisted. A hundred feet perhaps . . .

He led me into a hidden drive of a cul-de-sac off to the side of the rift we had been traversing. I collapsed there and everything began to swirl and ebb.

I thought I heard him say, "I am going now. Wait here."

"Sure thing," I seemed to reply.

Another blackness. Absolute. A parched, brittle thing/place of indeterminate size/duration. I was in it and vice-versa— equally distributed and totally contained by/in the nightmare system with consciousness at C^-" and chillthirstheatchillthirstheat a repeating decimal running every/anywhere on the projective plane that surrounded . . .

49

Flashes and imaginings . . . "Do you hear me, Fred? Do you hear me, Fred?" Water, trickling down my throat. Another blackness. Flash. Water, on my face, in my mouth. Movement. Shadows. A moaning . . .

Moaning. Shadows, a lesser black. Flash. Flashes. A light through parted lashes, dim. The ground below, passing. The moaning, mine.

"Do you hear me, Fred?"

"Yes," I said, "yes . . ."

The movement ceased. I overheard an exchange in a language I did not recognize. Then the ground rose. I was deposited upon it.

"Are you awake? Can you hear me?"

"Yes, yes. I already said 'yes.' How many times—"

"Yes, he appears to be awake"—this superfluous comment in a voice I recognized as that of my friend the wombat.

There had been more than one voice, but I could not see the speakers because of the angle at which I lay. And it was too much trouble to turn my head. I opened my eyes fully, though, and saw that the terrain was flat and pinked, though not tenderized, by the first low flames of morning.

All of the previous day's happenings slowly emerged from that place where memories stay when you are not using them. These, along with the moral I had drawn from them, were as responsible as muscle tone for my unwillingness to turn and regard my companions. And it wasn't bad just lying there. If I waited long enough, I might go away again and come back someplace else.

"I say," came a strange voice, "would you care for a peanut-butter sandwich?"

Pieces of broken reverie fell all about me. Gagging, I gained a new perspective on the ground and the long shadows that lay across it.

Because of the peculiar outline I had regarded, I was not completely surprised when I raised my head and saw a six-foot-plus kangaroo standing beside the wombat. It considered me through a pair of dark glasses as it removed a sandwich bag from its pouch.

"Peanut butter is rich in protein," it said.

4

HANGING THERE, some twenty or thirty thousand miles above it, I was in a perfect position to enjoy the event if California were to break loose, slip away and vanish beneath the Pacific. Unfortunately, this did not occur. Instead, the whole world slipped away as the vessel continued its orbiting and the argument proceeded behind my back.

However, at the rate things were going it seemed possible that the San Andreas fault would have several more opportunities to present me with the desired spectacle while providing some Donnelly of the distant future with material for a book on the peculiarities of that antediluvian world and its masterfully scripted passage. When one has nothing better to do one can always hope.

As, through that port beside which I reclined, presumably resting, only half listening to the heated sounds exchanged between Charv and Ragma, I regarded the Earth and then the star-dotted field beyond it, immense in the distance of distances, I was taken by a glorious sensation doubtless compiled of recovery from my earlier discomforts, a near-metaphysical satisfaction of my acrophiliac tendencies and a general overlay of fatigue that spread slowly, lightly across me, like a delicious fall of big-flaked snow. I had never been at this altitude before, witnessing the distances, struggling to gain perspective, over-whelmed by the consideration of space, space and more space. The beauty of basic things, things as they are and things as they might be, reached out to me then, and I recalled some lines I had scribbled long ago, on regretfully giving up my math major rather than take a degree in it:

Lobachevsky alone has looked on Beauty bare.
She curves in here, she curves in here. She curves out there.
Her parallel clefts come together to tease
In un-callipygianous-wise;
With fewer than one hundred eighty degrees
Her glorious triangle lies.
Her double-trumpet symmetry Riemann did not court—
His tastes to simpler-curvedness, the buxom Teuton sort!
An ellipse is fine for as far as it goes,
But modesty, away!
If I'm going to see Beauty without her clothes
Give me hyperbolas any old day.

The world is curves, I've heard it said,
And straightway in it nothing lies.
This then my wish, before I'm dead:
To look through Lobachevsky's eyes.

I felt very drowsy. I had been into and out of consciousness periodically and had no idea as to how much time had elapsed. My watch, of course, was of no assistance. I resisted going away again, however, both to prolong the aesthetic seizure and to keep abreast of developments about me.

I was uncertain as to whether my rescuers were aware of my wakefulness, in that I was facing away from them, reclined and loosely restrained in a hammocklike affair of soft webbing. And even if they were aware, the fact that they were conversing in a non-terrestrial language doubtless provided them with a feeling of insulation. At some earlier time I had slowly realized that the thing that would most have surprised them probably surprised me even more. This was the discovery that, when I gave it a piece of my divided attention, I could understand what they were saying.

A difficult phenomenon to describe better, but I'll try: If I listened intently to their words, they swam away from me, as elusive as individual fish in a school of thousands. If I simply regarded the waters, however, I could follow the changing outline, the drift, pick out the splashes and sparklings. Similarly, I could tell what they were saying. Why this should be I had no idea.

And I had ceased to care after a time, for their dialogue was quite repetitious. It was considerably more rewarding to consider the curtate cycloid described by Mount Chimborazo if one were positioned somewhere above the South Pole, to see this portion of the surface as moving backward with respect to the orbital progression of the body.

My thoughts suddenly troubled me. Where had that last one really come from? It felt beautiful, but was it mine? Had some valve given way in my unconscious, releasing a river of libido that cut big chunks of miscellanea from the banks it rushed between, to deposit them in shiny layers of silt up front here where I normally take my ease? Or could it be a telepathic phenomenon—me in a psychically defenseless position, two aliens the only other minds for thousands and thousands of miles about? Was one of them a logophile?

But it did not *seem* that way. I was certain that my comprehension of the language, for example, was not a telepathic thing. Their speech kept coming into better and better focus—individual words and phrases now, not just abstractions of their sense. I knew that language somehow, the sounds' meanings. I was not simply reading their minds.

What then?

Feeling more than a little sacrilegious, I forced the sense of peace and pleasure transcendent out to arms' length, then shoved as hard as I could. Think, damn it! I ordered my cortex. You are on overtime. Double time for holidays of the spirit. Move!

Turning and returning, back to the thirst, the chill, the aches, the morning . . . Yes. Australia. There I was . . .

The wombat had convinced the kangaroo, whose name I later learned was Charv, that water would benefit me more at that moment than a peanut-butter sandwich. Charv acknowledged the wombat's superior wisdom in matters of human physiology and located a flask in his pouch. The wombat, whose name I then learned to be Ragma, yanked off his paws—or, rather, pawlike mittens—displaying tiny, six-digited hands, thumb opposing, and he administered the liquid in slow doses. While this was being done, I gathered that they were alien plainclothesmen passing as local fauna. The reason was not clear.

"You are very fortunate—" Ragma told me.

After I finished choking, "I begin to appreciate the term 'alien viewpoint,' " I said, "I take it you are a member of a race of masochists."

"Some beings thank another who saves their life," he replied. "And I was about to complete the statement, 'You are very fortunate that we happened along this way.' "

"I'll give you the first," I said. "Thanks. But coincidence is like a rubber band. Stretch it too far and it snaps. Forgive me if I suspect some design in our meeting as we did."

"I am distressed that you focus suspicions upon us," he said, "when all that we have done is render assistance. Your cynicism index may be even higher than was indicated."

"Indicated by whom?" I asked.

"I am not permitted to say," he replied.

He cut short a snappy rejoinder by pouring more water down my throat. Choking and considering, I modified it to "This is ridiculous!"

"I agree," he said. "But now that we are here, everything should soon be in order."

I rose, stretched hard, pulled some of the kinks out of my muscles, seated myself on a nearby rock to defeat a small dizziness.

"All right," I said, reaching for a cigarette and finding all of them crushed. "How about your considering whatever you are permitted to say and then saying it?"

Charv withdrew a package of cigarettes—my brand—from his pouch and passed it to me.

"If you must," he said.

I nodded, opened it, lit one.

"Thank you," I said, returning them.

"Keep the pack," he said. "I am a pipe smoker of sorts. You, by the way, are more in need of rest and nourishment than nicotine. I am monitoring your heartbeat, blood pressure and basal metabolism rate on a small device I have with me—"

"Don't let it worry you, though," said Ragma, helping himself to a cigarette and producing a light from somewhere. "Charv is a hypochondriac. But I do think we ought to get back to our vessel before we talk. You are still not out of danger."

"Vessel? What sort? Where is it?"

"About a quarter of a mile from here," Charv offered, "and Ragma is correct. It will be safer if we depart this place immediately."

"I'll have to take your word for it," I said. "But you were looking for me—me specifically—weren't you? You knew my name. You seem to know something about me . . ."

"Then you have answered your own question," Ragma replied. "We had reason to believe you were in danger and we were correct."

"How? How did you know?"

They glanced at each other.

"Sorry," Ragma said. "That's another."

"Another what?"

"Thing we are not permitted to say."

"Who does your permitting and forbidding?"

"That's another."

I sighed. "Okay. I guess I'm up to walking that far. If I'm not, you'll know in a hurry."

"Very good," said Charv as I got to my feet.

I felt steadier this time up, and it must have been apparent. He nodded, turned and began moving away with a very unkangaroolike gait. I followed, and Ragma remained at my side. He maintained a bipedal posture this time.

The terrain was fairly level, so the going was not too bad. After a couple of minutes' movement, I was even able to work up some enthusiasm at the thought of the peanut-butter sandwich. Before I could comment on my improved condition, however, Ragma shouted something in Alienese.

Charv responded and took off at an accelerated pace, almost tripping over the lower extremities of his disguise.

Ragma turned to me. "He is going ahead to warm things up," he said, "for a quick liftoff. If you are capable of moving faster, please do so."

I complied as best I could, and "Why the rush?" I inquired.

"My hearing is quite sensitive," he said, "and I have just detected the fact that Zeemeister and Buckler are now airborne. This would seem to indicate that they are either looking for you or departing. It is always best to plan for the worst."

"I take it that they are my uninvited guests and that their names are something you are permitted to say. What do they represent?"

"They are doodlehums."

"Doodlehums?"

"Antisocial individuals, intentional circumventors of statutes."

"Oh, hoodlums. Yes, I guessed that much on my own. What can you tell me about them?"

"Morton Zeemeister," he said, "indulges in many such activities. He is the heavy one with the pale fur. Normally, he remains away from the scene of his hoodling, employing agents to execute it for him. The other, Jamie Buckler, is one such. He has hoodled well for Zeemeister over the years and was recently promoted by him to guard his body."

My own body was protesting the increased pace at that point, so I was not immediately certain whether the humming in my ears was the product of a tidal bore in my river of red stuff or the sound of the sinister bird. Ragma removed all doubt.

"They are coming this way," he said, "quite rapidly. Are you able to run?"

"I'll try," I said, forcing myself.

The ground dipped, rose again. Ahead, then, I was able to make out what I took to be their vessel: a squashed bell of dull metal, duller squares that might be ports spotted irregularly about its perimeter, an opened hatch . . . My lungs were working like a concertina at a Polish wedding and I felt the first spray of the tide of darkness within my head. I was going to go under again, I knew.

Then came that familiar flicker, as of having taken a step back from reality. I knew that my blood was pooling in my guts, leaving me high and dry, and I resented my subservience to the hydraulics involved. I heard gunshots above the growing roar, as on the soundtrack for a distant show, and even this was not sufficient to draw me back. When your own adrenalin lets you down, who is there left to trust?

I wanted very badly to make it to that hatch and through it. It was not all that distant. I knew now that I would not. An absurd way to die. This near, and not understanding anything . . .

"I'm going!" I shouted toward the bounding form at my side, not knowing whether the words really came out that way.

The sounds of gunfire continued, tiny as elfin popcorn. Fewer than forty feet remained, I was certain, as I judge local distances in terms of horseshoe-court lengths. Raising my arms to shield my face, I fell, not knowing whether I had been hit, scarcely able to care, forward, into a smooth blank that canceled the ground, the sound, the trouble, my flight.

Thus, thus, so and thus: awakening as a thing of textures and shadings: advancing and retreating along a scale of soft/dark, smooth/shadow, slick/bright: all else displaced and translated to this: the colors, sounds and balances a function of these two.

Advance to hard and very bright. Fall back to soft and black . . .

"Do you hear me, Fred?"—the twilight velvet.

"Yes"—my glowing scales.

"Better, better, better . . ."

"What/who?"

"Closer, closer, that not a sound betray . . ."

"There?"

"Better, that cease the subvocals . . ."

"I do not understand."

"Later for that. But one thing, a thing to say: Article 7224, Section C. Say it."

"Article 7224, Section C. Why?"

"If they wish to take you away—and they will—say it. But not why. Remember."

"Yes, but—"

"Later for that . . ."

A thing of textures and shadings: bright, brighter, smooth, smoother. Hard. Clear.

Lying there in my sling during Wakeful Period One:

"How are you feeling now?" Ragma asked.

"Tired, weak, still thirsty."

"Understandable. Here, drink this."

"Thanks. Tell me what happened. Was I hit?"

"Yes, you were hit twice. Fairly superficial. We have repaired the damage. The healing should be complete in a matter of hours."

"Hours? How many have passed since we departed?"

"Three, approximately, I carried you aboard after you fell. We lifted off, leaving your assailants, the continent, the planet, behind. We are in orbit about your world now, but we will be departing it shortly."

"You must be stronger than you look to have carried me."

"Apparently so."

"Where do you intend taking me from here?"

"To another planet—a most congenial one. The name would mean nothing to you."

"Why?"

"Safety and necessity. You seem to be in a position to provide information that could be very helpful in an investigation with which we are connected. We wish to obtain that information, but there are others who would like to have it also. Because of them, you would be in danger on your own planet. So, for purposes of insuring your safety as well as furthering our inquiry, the simplest thing is to remove you."

"Ask me. I'm not ungrateful for the rescue. What do you want to know? If it is the same thing Zeemeister and Buckler wanted, though, I'm afraid I can't be of much help."

"We are operating under that assumption. We believe that the information we require of you exists at an unconscious level, however. The best means of extracting something of that sort is through the offices of a good telepathic analyst. There are many such in the place we will be visiting."

"How long will we be there?"

"You will remain there until we have completed our investigation."

"And how long will that take?"

He sighed and shook his head.

"At this point it is impossible to say."

I felt the soft blackness brush like the tail of a passing cat against me. Not yet! No . . . I couldn't just let them haul me off that way for an indefinite leave of absence from everything I knew. It was in that moment that I appreciated the deathbed peeve—loose ends, all the little things that should be wrapped up before you go away: write that letter, settle up those accounts, finish the book on the night table . . . If I dropped out at this point in the semester, it would screw me up academically, financially—and who would buy my explanation? No. I had to stop them from taking me away. But the smooth to soft shadings were on the rise once more. I had to be quick.

"I'm sorry," I managed, "but that is impossible. I can't go with . . ."

"I am afraid that you must. It is absolutely necessary," he said.

"No," I said, panicking, fighting against fading before I could settle this. "No—you can't."

"I believe a similar concept exists in your own jurisprudence. You call it 'protective custody.' "

"What about Article 7224, Section C?" I blurted out, feeling my speech slip over into a slur as my eyes fell closed.

"What did you say?"

"You heard me," I remember muttering. "Seven . . . two . . . two . . . four. Sec . . . tion . . . C . . . That's why . . ."

And then, again, nothing.

The cycles of awareness bore me back—to consciousness or within spitting distance of it—several times more before I stuck at something approaching full wakefulness and filled it with California-watching. It was by degrees that I became aware of the argument that filled the air, obtaining its content in a detached, academic sort of way. They were upset over something that I had said.

Oh yes . . .

Article 7224, Section C. It had to do, I gathered, with the removal of intelligent creatures from their home planets without their consent. Part of a galactic treaty to which my rescuers' worlds were signatory, it was the closest thing to an interstellar constitution that they had. There was, however, sufficient ambiguity in the present situation to make for a debatable issue, in that there was also provision for removal without consent for a variety of overriding causes, such as quarantine for species protection, non-military reprisal for violations of certain other provisions, a kind of sensitive catchall for "interstellar security" and several more along these lines, all of which they discussed and rediscussed at great length. I had obviously touched on a delicate area, especially in light of the recency of their initial contact with Earth. Ragma kept insisting that if they chose one of the exceptions as controlling and removed me on that basis, their legal department would back them up. If it ever actually came to a point where an adjudication became necessary and they were reversed, he felt that he and Charv would not be held especially liable for their interpretation of the law, in that they were field operatives rather than trained legal personnel. Charv, meanwhile, maintained that it was obvious that none of the exceptions applied and that it would be even more obvious what they had done. Better, he decided, to let the telepathic analyst they employed implant the desire to cooperate within my mind. There were several, he was certain, who could be persuaded to solve their problem in that fashion. But this irritated Ragma. It would be a clear violation of my rights under another provision, as well as concealment of the evidence of their violation under this one. He would have no part of it. If they were going to move me, he wanted a defense other than concealment. So they reviewed the exceptions again, pondering each word, letting the words talk to each other, recalling past cases, sounding the while like Jesuits, Talmudists, dictionary editors or disciples of the New Criticism. We continued to orbit the Earth.

It was not until much later that Charv interrupted things with a question that had been bothering me all along: "Where did he learn about Article 7224, anyway?"

They repaired to the sling, interrupting my view of storm patterns off Cape Hatteras. Seeing that my eyes were open, they nodded and gestured in what I believe they intended as a pantomime of good will and concern.

"Have you been resting well?" Charv inquired.

"Quite."

"Water?"

"Please."

I drank some, then: "Sandwich?" he asked.

"Yes. Thanks."

He produced one and I began eating.

"We have been quite concerned over your well-being—and about doing the right thing in your case."

"That is good of you."

"We have been wondering about something that you said a while back, dealing with our offer to provide you with sanctuary during a fairly routine investigation we will be conducting on your planet. It seemed as if you cited a section of the

Galactic Code just before you dropped off to sleep last time. But you mumbled somewhat and we could not be certain. Was this the case?"

"Yes."

"I see," he said, adjusting his sunglasses. "Would you mind telling us how you became acquainted with its provisions?"

"Such things travel quickly in academic circles," I offered, which was the best response I could locate in my supply of misleading statements.

"It is possible," said Ragma, dropping back into whatever they had been speaking earlier. "Their scholars have been working on translations. They may be completed by now and circulating about their universities. It is not my department, so I cannot be certain."

"And if somebody has put together a course on the subject, this one has probably taken it," said Charv. "Yes. Unfortunate."

"Then you must be aware," Charv continued, switching back to English and aiming it in my direction, "that your planet is not yet signatory to the agreement."

"Of course," I replied. "But then, my concern is really with your own actions under its provisions."

"Yes, of course," he said, glancing at Ragma.

Ragma moved nearer, his unblinking wombat eyes holding something like a glare.

"Mister Cassidy," he said, "let me put it as simply as possible. We are law officers—cops, if you like—with a job to do. I regret that we cannot give you the particulars, as it would probably make it much easier to obtain your cooperation. As it is, your presence on your planet would represent a distinct impediment to us, while your absence would make things considerably simpler. As we have already told you, if you remain you will be in some danger. Bearing this in mind, it seems obvious that we would both be best served if you would agree to a small vacation."

"I'm sorry," I said.

"Then perhaps," he went on, "I may appeal to your venality as well as your much-lauded primate adventuresomeness. A trip like this would probably cost you a fortune if you could arrange it yourself, and you would have an opportunity to see sights none of your kind has ever witnessed before."

It did get through to me, that. At any other time I would not have hesitated. But my feelings had just then sorted themselves out. It went without saying that something was amiss and that I was a part of it. But it was more than the world that was out of whack. Something that I did not understand had happened/was happening to me. I grew convinced that the only way I could discover it and remedy or exploit it was to stay home and do my own investigating. I was doubtful that anyone else's would serve my ends as I would have them served.

So: "I am sorry," I repeated.

He sighed, turned away, looked out the port and regarded the Earth.

Finally: "Yours is a very stubborn race," he said.

When I did not respond, he added, "But so is mine. We must return you if you insist. But I will find a way to achieve the necessary results without your cooperation."

"What do you mean?" I asked.

"If you are lucky," he said, "you may live to regret your decision."

5

HANGING THERE, tensing and untensing my muscles to counteract the pendulum effect of the long, knotted line, I examined the penny on which Lincoln faced to the left. It looked precisely the way a penny would look if I were regarding it in a mirror, reversed lettering and all. Only I was holding it in the palm of my hand.

Beside/below me, where I dangled but a couple of feet above the floor, hummed the Rhennius machine: three jet-black housings set in a line on a circular platform that rotated slowly in a counterclockwise direction, the end units each extruding a shaft—one vertical, one horizontal—about which passed what appeared to be a Moebius strip of a belt almost a meter in width, one strand half running through a tunnel in the curved and striated central unit, which faintly resembled a wide hand cupped as in the act of scratching.

Pumping my knees, feet braced against the terminal knot, I set up a gentle swaying that bore me, moments later, back above the ingoing aperture of the middle component. Lowering myself, extending my arm, I dropped the penny onto the belt, was halted at the end of my arc, began the return swing. Still crouched and reaching, I snared the penny as it emerged.

Not what I had expected. Not at all, and no indeed.

In that its first journey through the innards of the thing had reversed the coin, I had assumed that running it through the works again would return it to normal. Instead, I now held a metal disk on which the design was properly oriented but was incised, intaglio-like, rather than raised. This applied to both sides, and in the place of the milling the edges were step-recessed, like a train wheel.

Curiouser and curiouser. I would simply have to do it again to see what happened next. I straightened, gripped the line with my knees, began to redirect my errant arc.

For a moment I glanced up into the gloom where my thirty-foot puppet string reached to its shadowy bar. An I-beam, too near the ceiling to mount, I had traversed it aardvark-style—ankles locked above, letting my fingers do the walking. I wore a dark sweater and trousers and had on thin-soled suede boots. I had carried the line coiled about my left shoulder until I had reached a point as near to being directly above the apparatus as was possible.

I had made my way in through a skylight I had had to jimmy after cutting away some grillwork and jump-wiring three alarms in a fashion that produced a small nostalgia for my abandoned major in electrical engineering. The hall below was dim, the only illumination provided by a series of floor-level spots that encircled the display and concentrated their beams upward upon it. A low guardrail enclosed the machine, and concealed electric eyes fenced it invisibly. Sensor plates within the floor and the platform would betray a footstep. There was a television camera bolted to my beam. I had turned it slowly, slightly, so that it was still focussed on the display—only farther southward, as I planned to descend on the north side where the belt was flattest just before it reached the central unit—a guesstimate, from those four courses in TV production. There were guards in the building, but one had just made his rounds and

I planned to be quick. All plans have their limits and hazards, which is why insurance companies get rich.

The night was cloudy and a very cold wind went around in it. My breath flapped ghostly wings and flew away. The only witness to my finger-numbing exercises on the roof was a tired-looking cat crouched in the scuttleway. The chill had been about when I had arrived in town the night before, a journey resulting from a decision I had reached on Hal's couch the previous day.

After Charv and Ragma had, at my request, set me down about fifty miles out of town during the dark of the moon, I had hitched rides and gotten back to my neighborhood well after midnight. And a good thing it was that I had.

There is a side street that dead-ends into my own, and my building is right across the way from it. As you proceed along that side street the windows of my apartment are in plain sight. More naturally in night's dark and quiet than they would by day, my eyes sought them. Dark, as they should be. Blank. Vacant.

But then, half a minute later, as I neared the corner, came a small flare, a tiny flickering, blackness again.

Any other time and I would have dismissed it if I had noted it at all. It could very easily have been a reflection or an imagining. Yet . . .

Yes. But recently recuperated and still full of warnings, I would be a fool to be anything but wary. Neither a fool nor a raisin be, I told myself as I put on my waries, turned right and headed away.

I walked a pair of blocks to and a couple from, coming at last up the alley behind my building. There was a rear entranceway, but I avoided it, making my way to a place where I could go from pipe to sill to ledge to fire escape, which I did.

In a very brief while I was on the roof and moving across it. Then down the pipe to the place I had stood when talking with Paul Byler. I edged forward from there and peered in my bedroom window. Too dark to tell anything for certain. It was the other window, though, that had framed what might have been the lighting of a cigarette.

I rested my fingertips on the window, pressed firmly, then exerted a steady pressure upward. It slid open without a sound, the reward of consideration. Being an erratic sleeper and fond of my nighttime gambols, I kept the running grooves heavily waxed so as not to disturb my roommate.

Leaving my shoes behind on the ledge, I entered and stood still, ready to flee.

I waited a minute, breathing slowly, through my mouth. Quieter that way. Another minute . . .

A creak from my uneasy easy chair reached me, an effect it always manages when its occupant uncrosses and recrosses his legs.

That would place a person to the right of the desk in the front room, in a position near to the window.

"Is there any coffee in that thing?" a harsh voice managed softly.

"I think so" came the reply.

"Then pour me some."

Sounds of a thermos being unstoppered. Pouring. A few scrapes and bumps. A muttered "Thanks." They placed the other fellow at the desk itself.

A slurp. A sigh. The scratch of a match. More silence.

Then: "Wouldn't it be funny if he'd gotten himself killed?"

A snort.

"Yeah. Not bloody likely, though."

"How can you say that?"

"He stinks of luck, or something like it. And he's such an odd one to begin with."

"That I'll buy. Wish he'd hurry up and find his way home."

"That makes for two of us."

The one in the easy chair got to his feet and moved to the window. After a time he sighed. "How long, how long, O Lord?"

"It will be worth the wait."

"I'm not denying it. But the sooner we catch hold of him the better."

"Of course. I'll drink to that."

"Hear! What've you got there?"

"A bit of brandy."

"You've had that all along and you've been giving me this black mud?"

"You kept asking for coffee. Besides, I just found it a while back."

"Pass it here."

"There's another glass. Let's be genteel. It's good stuff."

"Pour!"

I heard the cork come out of my Christmas bottle. A few clinks followed and footfalls.

"Here you are."

"Smells good."

"Doesn't it?"

"To the Queen!"

A shuffling of feet. A single clink.

"God save 'er!"

They reseated themselves after that and grew silent once again. I stood there for perhaps a quarter of an hour, but nothing more was said.

So I edged my way to the corner rack, found some money I had left behind still in its place in the boot, removed it, pocketed it, removed myself back to the ledge.

I closed the window as carefully as I had opened it, retreated to the roof, cut across the path of a black cat who arched his back and spat—doubtless superstitious, not that I blamed him—and made my way away.

After scouting Hal's building for loiterers other than myself and not spotting any, I rang his place from the booth on the corner. I was somewhat surprised to have my call answered in a matter of seconds.

"Yeah?"

"Hal?"

"Yeah. Who's this?"

"Your old buddy who climbs things."

"Hoo boy! What kind of trouble are you in, anyway?"

"If I knew that I'd have something for my pains. Can you tell me anything about it?"

"Probably nothing important. But there are some small things that might—"

"Listen, may I come over?"

"Sure, why not?"

"Now, I mean. I hate to be a bother, but—"

"No trouble. C'mon up."

"Are you all right?"

"Matter of fact, no. Mary and I had a little difference of opinion and she's spending the weekend at her mother's. I'm half stoned, which leaves me half sober. Which is enough. You tell me your troubles and I'll tell you mine."

"It's a deal. I'll be there in half a minute."

"Great. See you then."

So I cradled it, walked over, went in, buzzed his number and got admitted. Moments later I was knocking on his door.

"Prompt, oh prompt," he said, swinging it wide and stepping aside. "Enter, pray."

"In which order?"

"Oh, bless this house, by all means, first. It could use a little grace."

"Bless," I said, stepping in. "Sorry to hear you got troubles."

"They'll pass. It started out with a burnt dinner and being late for a show, that's all. Stupid thing. I thought it was her when the phone rang. I guess I'll have to do my apologizing tomorrow. The hangover should make me sound exceptionally repentant. What're you drinking?"

"I don't really . . . Oh, what the hell! Whatever you've got there."

"A drop of soda in a sea of Scotch."

"Make it the other way around," I said, moving on into the living room and settling in a big, soft, tilted chair.

Moments later Hal came in, handed me a tall glass from which I took a healthy slug, sat down across from me, tasted his own, then said, "Have you committed any especially monstrous acts lately?"

I shook my head.

"Always the victim, never the victor. What have you heard?"

"Nothing, really. It's all been implication and inference. People have been asking me a lot about you but not telling me much."

"People? Who?"

"Well, your adviser Dennis Wexroth was one—"

"What did he want?"

"More information about your individual project in Australia."

"Like, for instance?"

"Like where. He wanted to know exactly where you were digging around."

"What did you tell him?"

"That I didn't know, which was reasonably true. This was over the phone. Then he stopped by in person, and he had a man along with him—a Mister Nadler. The guy had an I.D. card saying he was an employee of the State Department. He acted as if they were concerned about the possibility of your removing artifacts from over there and creating an incident."

I said something vulgar.

"Yeah, that's what I thought, too," he said. "He pressed me to rack my memory for anything you might have said concerning your itinerary. I was tempted to misremember, say, Tasmania. Got scared, though. Didn't know what they could do. So I just kept insisting you hadn't told me anything of your plans."

"Good. When did this happen?"

"Oh, you'd been gone for over a week. I'd gotten your post-card from Tokyo."

"I see. That's it, then?"

"Hell, no. That was just the beginning."

I took another big swallow.

"Nadler was back the next day, asking whether I'd remembered anything else. He'd already given me a number to call if I did, or if I heard from you. So I was irritated. I said no and got rid of him. Then he came around again this morning to impress on me that it was to your benefit if I cooperated, that you might be in trouble and that I could help you by being honest. By the time they had learned of your difficulties at the Sydney Opera House, he said, you'd disappeared into the desert. What happened at the Sydney Opera House anyway?"

"Later, later. Get on with it. Or is that all?"

"No, no. I got irritated again, told him no again and that was all so far as he was concerned. But there were other inquiries. I received at least half a dozen phone calls from people who claimed they just had to get in touch with you, that it was very important. None of them would say why, though. Or give me anything that could be used to trace them."

"What do you mean? Did you try tracing them?"

"No, but the detective did."

"Detective?"

"I was just getting to that part. This place has been broken into and ransacked on three separate occasions during the past two weeks. Naturally, I called the cops. I didn't see any connection with the calls, but after the third time the detective wanted me to tell him about anything unusual that had happened recently. So I mentioned that strange people kept calling and asking for a friend who was out of town. Several of them had left numbers, and he thought it was worth looking into. I talked with him yesterday, though, and he said nothing had turned up. All of them were from semipublic phones."

"Was anything stolen?"

"No. That bothered him, too."

"I see," I said, sipping slowly. "Has anyone approached you directly with unusual questions not involving me? Specifically, about that stone of Byler's?"

"No. But you might be interested in knowing that his lab was broken into while you were away. No one could really tell whether anything was missing. Getting back to your other question, though, while nobody approached me about the stone, someone seemed to be getting near for some purpose or other. Maybe it was tied in with the entry and searching here. I don't know. But for several days it seemed that I was being followed about. I didn't pay much attention at first. Actually, it wasn't until things started happening that I thought of him. The same man, not especially obtrusive, but always around—somewhere. Never came near enough for me to get a good look. At first I thought I was just being neurotic. Later, of course, he came to mind. Too late, though. He disappeared after the police started paying attention to me and to this building."

He tossed off the rest of his drink and I finished mine.

"That pretty much summarizes things," he said. "Let me fix us a couple more of these, then you tell me what you know."

"Go ahead."

I lit a cigarette and pondered. There had to be a pattern to all this, and it seemed likely that the star-stone was the key. There were too many subsidiary actions to try to separate, analyze, follow up individually. If I knew more about the stone, though, I felt that these recent happenings might begin to drift into truer perspective. Thus began my list of priorities.

Hal returned with the drinks, gave me mine, reseated himself.

"All right," he said, "considering everything that's been happening here, I'm ready to believe anything you've got to tell me."

So I told him most of what had occurred since my departure.

"I don't believe you," he said when I had finished.

"I can't lend you my memories in any better condition."

"Okay, okay," he said "It's weird. But then, so are you. No offense. Let me fog my brain a little more and I'll try to consider it. Right back."

He went and freshened the drinks again. I was beyond caring. I had lost count during the time I'd been talking.

"You were being serious?" he finally said.

"Yes."

"Then those fellows are probably still back at the apartment."

"Possibly."

"Why not call the police?"

"Hell, for all I know they may *be* the police."

"Toasting the Queen that way?"

"Could be their old alma mater's Homecoming Queen. I don't know. I'd just as soon no one knew I'm back till I've learned more and done more thinking."

"Okay. Silence here. What can I do to help?"

"Think. You've been known to have an original idea every now and then. Come up with one."

"All right," he said. "I have been thinking about it. Everything seems to go back to the star-stone facsimile. What is it about the thing that makes it so important?"

"I give up. Tell me."

"I don't know. But let's consider everything that is known about it."

"Okay. The original came to us on loan as part of that cultural exchange deal we've joined. It was described as a relic, a specimen of unknown utility—but most likely decorative—found among the ruins of a dead civilization. Seems to be synthetic. If so, it may be the oldest intelligently fashioned object in the galaxy."

"Which makes it priceless."

"Naturally."

"If it were lost or destroyed here, we could be kicked out of the exchange program."

"I suppose that is possible . . ."

" 'Suppose,' hell! We can. I looked it up. The library now has a full translation of the agreement, and I got curious enough to see what it said. A hearing would be held, and the other members would vote on the matter of our expulsion."

"Good thing it hasn't been lost or destroyed."

"Yeah. Great."

"How could Byler have gotten access to it?"

"My guess is still the UN itself—that they approached him to create a duplicate for display purposes, he did it and then there was a mixup."

"I can't see the mixup on something that important."

"Then suppose it was intentional."

"How so?"

"Say they loaned it to him, and instead of returning the original and a copy he returned two copies. I can see him as wanting to hang onto it and study it for as long as he could. He could have given it back when he was finished or caught, whichever came first, and claimed he had made a simple error. No fuss could be raised, with the entire enterprise that clandestine. Or perhaps I am being too devious. Maybe he'd had it on a legitimate loan all the while, studying it at their request. Whichever, let us suppose that he'd had the original up until a while back."

"All right, say that."

"Then it vanished. Either it got mixed in and thrown out with some of the inferior replicas, or it was the one given to us in error . . ."

"To you, to you," I said, "and not in error."

"Paul arrived at this conclusion, too," he continued, ignoring the assignment of guilt. "He panicked, went looking and roughed us up in the process."

"What precipitated his wising up?"

"Someone spotted the ringer and asked him for the real one. When he looked it wasn't there."

"And he got dead."

"You said the two men who questioned you in Australia as much as admitted having done him in as a by-product of questioning him."

"Zeemeister and Buckler. Yes."

"The undercover wombat told you they were hoodlums."

"Doodlehums, but go ahead."

"The UN informed the member nations—which is where the State Department comes into the picture in our case. Somewhere there was a tear in the bean-bag, though, and Zeemeister decided to locate the stone first in order to claim a large ransom. Pardon me, a reward."

"It does make a kind of surrealistic sense. Continue."

"So we might have had it and everybody knows it. We don't know where it is, but nobody believes us."

"Who is everybody?"

"UN officials, the Foggy Bottom boys, the doodlehums and the aliens."

"Well, granting that the aliens have been informed and are actually assisting in the investigation, Charv and Ragma become a little more understandable—with their thing about security and all. But then, something else bothers me. They seemed awfully sure that I knew more than I thought I did concerning the stone's whereabouts. They even felt that a telepathic analyst might turn up some useful leads in my subconscious. I wonder what gave them that idea?"

"You've got me there. Perhaps they have eliminated almost everything else. And maybe they are right. It did seem to vanish rather strangely. I wonder . . .?"

"What?"

"If you do know something useful, something you may have suppressed for some reason? Perhaps a good nontelepathic analyst could drag it out, too. Hypnosis, drugs . . . Who knows? What about that Doctor Marko you used to go to?"

"It's a thought, but it would take a long while to convince him as to the reality of all the preliminaries he'd need to know before he could go to work. Might even think I've lost touch, trank me up and give me the wrong therapy. No. I'll hold off on that angle for now."

"Where does that leave us?"

"Drunk," I said. "My higher cerebral centers all just moved off center."

"Want me make some coffee?"

"No. Consciousness is losing six to nothing and I'd like to retire gracefully. Mind if I sleep on the couch?"

"Go ahead. I'll get you a blanket and a pillow."

"Thanks."

"Maybe we'll have some fresh ideas in the morning," he said, rising.

"Thinking them will be painful, whatever they are," I said, going over to the couch and kicking off my shoes. "Let there be an end to thought. Thus do I refute Descartes."

I sprawled, not a cogito or a sum to my name.

Obliv—

There was a teletype machine in a room at the back of my mind. It had never been used. Within the uncreation where the not-I didn't exist for a peaceful interval of non-time, however, it stuttered and spewed, synthesizing some recipient who resembled myself for purposes of pestering him . . .

```
: : : : : : : : : : : : : : : : : : : : : : : : : : : : : : : : : : : : :
: : : : DO YOU HEAR ME, FRED? : : : : : : : : : : : : : : : : : :
: : : : : : : : : : : : : : : : : : : : : : : : : : : : : : : : : : : : : :
: : : : : : : : : : : : : : : : : : : : : : : : : : : : : : : : : : : : : :
: : : : : : : : : : : : : : : : : : : : DO YOU HEAR ME, FRED? :
: : : : : : : : : : : : : : : : : : : : : : : : : : : : : : : : : : : : : :
: : : : : : : : : : : : : : : : : : : : : : : : : : : : : : : : : : YES :
: : : : : : : : : : : : : : : : : : : : : : : : GOOD : : : : : : : : :
: : : : : WHO ARE YOU? : : : : : : : : : : : : : : : : : : : : : : :
: I AMXXXXXXXXXXXXXXXX : DO YOU HEAR ME, : : : : :
FRED? : : : : : : : : : : : : : : : : : : : : : : : : : : : : : : : : : :
: : : : : : : : : : : : : : : : : : : : YES. WHO ARE YOU? : : : :
: : : : I AMXXXXXX IXXXXXXX ARTICLE 7224
SECTION C. I BROUGHT IT TO YOUR ATTENTION
: : : : : : : : : : : : : : : : : : : : : : : : ALL RIGHT : : : : : : :
: : : : : : : : : : : : : : : : : : : : : : : : : : : : : : : : : : : : : :
: : : : : : : : : : : : : : : : : : : : : : : : : : : : : : : : : : : : : :
: CAN YOU OBTAIN AN N-AXIAL INVERSION
UNIT? : : : : : : : : : : : : : : : : : : : : : : : : : : : : : : : : : :
```

NO

IT IS IMPORTANT

IT IS ALSO UNDEFINED

NECESSARY

WHAT THE HELL IS AN N-AXIAL INVERSION UNIT?

TIME NAMES CORRESPONDENCESXXXXXXXX XXXXXXXX THE RHENNIUS MACHINE. THAT MECHANISM

I KNOW WHERE IT IS. YES

GO TO THE RHENNIUS MACHINE. TEST ITS INVERSION PROGRAM

HOW?

OBSERVE THE PROGRESSIVE TRANSFORMATIONS OF AN OBJECT PASSED THROUGH ITS MOBILATOR

WHAT IS A MOBILATOR?

THE CENTRAL UNIT THROUGH WHICH ITS BELT MOVES

IMPOSSIBLE TO GET THAT CLOSE TO THE THING. IT IS UNDER GUARD

VITAL

WHY?

TO REFORMULATEXXXXXXXXXXXXXXXXXXX TO REFORMXXXXXXXXXXXXXXXX TOXXX XXXXX

DO YOU HEAR ME, FRED?

YES

: : : : : : : : GO TO THE RHENNIUS MACHINE AND TEST
ITS INVERSION PROGRAM :
SUPPOSING I CAN DO IT. WHAT THEN? : : : : : : : : : : : :
: : : : : : : : : : THEN GO AND GET DRUNK : : : : : : : : : :
: :
: : : : : : : : : : : : : : : : : : PLEASE REPEAT : : : : : : : : : :
: : TEST   THE   INVERSION   PROGRAM   AND   GO
INTOXICATE YOURSELF :
: :
: ANYTHING ELSE? : : :
: : : : : : : : : SUBSEQUENT ACTIONS CONTINGENT UPON
UNDETERMINED EVENTS :
: :
: :
: :
: WILL YOU DO THIS? :
: WHO ARE YOU? : : :
: :
: : : : : : : : I   XXXXXXXXXXXXXXSPEICUSXXXXXXXXXXXX
XXXSPEICUSXXXXXXX :
XXXXSPEICUSPEICUSPEICUSPEICUSPEICUSP EICUSPEICU
SPEICUSXXXXXXXXXXXXXXXXX XXXXXXXXXXXXXXXXXX
XXXXXXXEICUSPEIXXCUSPEXXICUSXXXXXXXXXX XXXX
XXXPECXXXUSPEIXXXXCUSPEICUSPEICUSPEICUSPEICU
SPEICUSPEICUSPEICUSPEICUSPEICUSPEICUSPEICUSPEIC
USXXXXXXXXXXXXXXXXXXXXXXXXXXXXXX XXXXXXXXX
XXXXXXXXXXXXXXXXXXXXXXXXXXXXXXXXXXXXXXXXX
XXXXXX XXXXXXXXXXXXXXXXXXXXXXXXXXXXXXXXXXXX
XXXXXXXXXXXXXXXXXI AM A RECORDINGXXXSPEICUS
XXXXXXXXXXI AM A RECORDINGXXXSPEICUS XXXXXXX
XXXI AM A RECORDINGXX :
: :
: :
: IT FIGURES : : : : : : : : :
: :

: : : : : : : WILL YOU DO AS I HAVE ASKED? : : : : : : : : :
: :
: WHY NOT? : : : : : :
: :
: : YOU INDICATE ASSENT? :
: : : : : : : : : : : : : ALL RIGHT, RECORDING. ALL RIGHT.
AFFIRMATIVE. I AM PROGRAMMED CURIOUS : : : : : : :
: :
: : : : : : : : : : : : : : VERY GOOD. THAT THEN IS ALLOO
OOOOOOOOOOOOOOOOOOOOOOOOOOOOOOOOOOOOOOOOO
O: :
OOOOOOOOOOOOOOOOOOOOOOOOOOOOOOOOOOOOOOOOO
O: :
OOOOOOOOOOOOOOOOOOOOOOOOOOOOOOOOOOOOOOOOO
O: :
OOOOOOOOOOOOOOOOOOOOOOOOOOOOOOOOOOOOOOO
O —ion.

It raineth on the just and the unjust; likewise shineth the sun. I came around with the latter doing that thing, in my eyes, through the front window. And I must have been just—or just lucky—as I was not only unhung over but felt fairly good. I lay there for some time, listening to Hal's snores coming from the other room. Reaching a decision as to who and where I was, I rose and set a pot of coffee to gurgling in the kitchen and went to the bathroom to find some soap and a razor and do some other things.

Later, I had some juice, toast and a couple of eggs, took a cup of coffee back to the living room. Hal was still buzzing. I loafed on the sofa. I lit a cigarette. I drank coffee.

Caffeine, nicotine, the games the blood sugars play—I do not know what it was that pierced the dark bubble as I sat there assembling the morning and myself.

Whatever prompted it, the thing I had gotten in lieu of the usual unsolicited dreams returned to me between a puff and a sip, far clearer than my idsponsored late late monster shows ever were.

Having decided earlier to accept the peculiar in the proper spirit, I confined my considerations to the matter of content. It made as much sense as any of a number of things I had recently experienced, and possessed the virtue of requiring a positive action on my part at a time when I was weary of being acted upon.

So I folded the blankets and placed them in a neat heap with the pillow on top. I finished my coffee, poured a second cup and turned the pot down to a simmer. I located some writing paper atop a miscellaneous chest of drawers and scrawled a note: "Hal—Thanks. I've a thing I'm off to pursue. It came to me last night. Quite peculiar. Will call in a day or so & let you know what comes of it. Hope everything is happily ever after again by then.—Fred. P.S. The coffee is on." Which covered everything I could think of. I left it on the other end of the sofa.

I got out and headed for the bus station. A long ride lay ahead. I would arrive too late, but the next day I would see the Rhennius machine during normal viewing hours and figure a way to get at it for a private showing later on.

And I did.

Voila! Lincoln stared to my right again and everything else seemed in its proper place. I pocketed the cent, steadied myself, began to climb.

Halfway up, brassy bongs bloomed in my ears, my nervous system came unzipped and my arms turned to putty. The free end of the line was swinging widely. Perhaps it had struck something, or gotten into range of the camera. Academic, whichever.

Moments later, I heard a shouted, "Raise your hands!" which probably came to mind a lot more readily, say, than "Stop climbing that rope and come back down without touching the machine!"

I did raise them, too, rapidly and repeatedly.

By the time he was threatening to shoot, I was across the beam and eyeing the window. If I could spring, catch hold, pull, vault, pass horizontally through the eighteen-inch opening I had left myself and hit the roof rolling, I would have a head start with a variety of high routes before me. I would have a chance.

I tensed my muscles.

"I'll shoot!" he repeated, almost directly beneath me now.

I heard the shot and there was glass in the air as I moved.

6

IT WAS THE SOUND OF THE STEAM, whistling through, rattling the ancient pipes, that drew me across the fine line to the place where identity surprises itself. I balked immediately and tried to go back, but the heating system wouldn't let me. In close-eyed preconsciousness I clung to the transitory pleasure of being without memory. Then I realized that I was thirsty. And then that something hard and uncomfortable was indenting my right side. I did not want to wake up.

But the circle of sensations widened, things fell together, the center held. I opened my eyes.

Yes . . .

I was lying on a mattress on the floor in the corner of a cluttered, gaudy room. Some of the clutter was magazines, bottles, cigarette butts and random articles of clothing; some of the gaud was paintings and posters that clung to the walls like stamps on a foreign parcel, bright and crooked. Strings of glass beads hung in a doorway to my right, catching what seemed like morning light from a large window directly across from me. A golden blizzard of dust fell through its rays, stirred perhaps by the donkey who was nibbling at the potted pot that occupied the window seat. From the sill, an orange cat blinked at me in yellow-eyed appraisal, then closed her eyes.

A few small traffic sounds came from a point beyond and below the window. Through the sun patterns on the streaked glass, I could make out the upper corner of a brick building sufficiently distant to indicate that a street did indeed lie between us. I made my first dry swallowing movement of the morning and realized again how thirsty I felt. The air was dry and rank with stale odors, some familiar, some exotic.

I shifted slightly, testing myself for aches. Not bad. A small throbbing from the frontal sinuses, not sufficient to herald a headache. I stretched then, feeling a fraction fitter.

I discovered the sharp object prodding my side to be a bottle, empty. I winced as I recalled how it had gotten that way. The party, oh yes . . . There had been a party . . .

I sat up. I saw my shoes. I put them on. I stood.

Water . . . There was a bathroom around the corner through the beads in the back. Yes.

Before I could move in that direction, the donkey turned, stared at me, advanced.

By a splinter of a second, I'd say, I saw what was coming, before it came.

"You are still fogged up," the donkey said, or seemed to say, the words ringing strangely in my head, "so go quench your thirst and wash your face. But do not use the window back there for an exit. It could result in difficulties. Please return to this room when you have finished. I have some things to tell you."

From a place beyond surprise, I said, "All right," and I went on back and ran the water.

There was nothing especially suspicious beyond the bathroom window. No one in sight to be the wiser, no one to do anything about it if I decided to cross over to the next building, then up, up and away. I had no intention of doing it just then, but it made me wonder whether the donkey might be something of an alarmist.

The window . . . My mind went back to that bar of black, to the snap of the gun, to the glass. I had torn my jacket on the frame and scraped my shoulder where I hit. I'd kept rolling, rolled to my feet and taken off running, crouched. . . .

An hour later I was in a bar in the Village carrying out the second part of my instructions. Not too quickly, though, as the fugitive feeling was still with me and I wanted to hang onto my faculties long enough to regroup myself emotionally. Consequently, I ordered a beer and sipped it slowly.

Small gusts of wind had been tumbling bits of paper along the streets. Random flakes of snow had angled by, turning to damp splotches wherever they touched. Later, the middle state was omitted and cold raindrops alternately sprayed, dripped, ceased altogether, drifted in patches of mist.

The wind whistled as it slipped about the door, and even with my jacket on I felt chilly. So ten or fifteen minutes later when I'd finished the beer, I went looking for a warmer bar. That was what I told myself, though from some more primitive level the flight impulse still operated, assisting in the decision.

I hit three more bars in the next hour, drinking one beer per and moving on. Along the way, I stopped in a package store and picked up a bottle, as it was late and I was loath to go too blotto in public. I began thinking about where I would spend the night. I'd get a taxi by and by, I decided, let the driver find me a hotel and complete the intoxication business there. No sense in speculating what the results would be and no need to hurry things along. At the moment I wanted people about me, their voices, walls that echoed a tinny music. While my last memories of Australia were messy and blurred, I had been brighteyed and strung tight as a tennis racket on departing the hall. I could still hear the snap and the brittle notes of the glass. It is not good to think about having been shot at.

The fifth bar that I hit was a happy find. Three or four steps below street level, warm, pleasantly dim, it contained sufficient patrons to satisfy my need for social noises but not so many that anyone begrudged my taking up a table against the far wall. I took off my jacket and lit a cigarette. I would stay awhile.

So it was there that he found me, half an hour or so later. I had succeeded in relaxing considerably, forgetting a bit and achieving a state of warmth and comfort, let the wind go whistle, when a passing figure halted, turned and settled onto the seat across from me.

I did not even look up. My peripheral vision told me it was not a cop and I did not feel like acknowledging an unsolicited presence, especially the likely weirdo.

We sat that way—unmoving—for almost half a barbed minute. Then something flashed on the tabletop and I looked down, automatically.

Three totally explicit photos lay before me: two brunettes and a blonde.

"How'd you like to warm up with something like that on a cold night like this?" came a voice that snapped my mind through years to alertness and my eyes forty-five degrees upward.

"Doctor Merimee!" I said.

"Ssh!" he hissed. "Pretend you're looking at the pictures!"

The same old trench coat, silk scarf and beret . . . The same long cigarette holder . . . Eyes of unbelievable magnitude behind glasses that still gave me the impression of peering into an aquarium. How many years had it been?

"What the devil are you doing here?" I said.

"Gathering material for a book, of course. Dammit! Look at the pictures, Fred! Pretend to study them. Really. Trouble afoot. Yours, I think."

So I looked back at the glossy ladies.

"What kind of trouble?" I said.

"There's a fellow seems to be following you."

"Where is he now?"

"Across the street. In a doorway last I saw him."

"What's he look like?"

"Couldn't really tell. He's dressed for the weather. Bulky coat. Hat pulled down. Head bent forward. Average height or a bit less. Possibly kind of husky."

I chuckled.

"Sounds like anybody. How do you know he's following me?"

"I caught sight of you over an hour ago, several bars back. That one was fairly crowded, though. Just as I'd started toward you, you got up to leave. I called out, but you didn't hear me over the noise. By the time I'd paid up and gotten out myself you were part way up the street. I started after you and saw this fellow come out of a doorway and do the same. I thought nothing of it at first, but you did wander awhile and he was making all the same turns. Then when you found another bar, he just stopped and stared at it. Then he went into a doorway, lit a cigar, coughed several times and waited there, watching the place. So I walked on by as far as the corner. There was a phone booth, and I got inside and watched him while I pretended to make a call. You didn't stay in that place very long, and when you came out and moved on, he did the same. I held off approaching you for two more bars, just to be positive. But I am convinced now. You are being followed."

"Okay," I said. "I buy that."

"Your casual acceptance of the situation causes me to believe that it was not wholly unexpected."

"Exactly."

"Does it involve anything I might be able to help you with?"

"Not in terms of the headache's causes. But possibly the immediate symptoms . . ."

"Like getting you away from here without his noting it?"

"That is what I had in mind."

He gestured with a bandaged hand.

"No problem. Take your time with your drink. Relax. Consider it done. Pretend to study the merchandise."

"Why?"

"Why not?"

"What happened to your hand?"

"Accident, sort of, with a butcher knife. Have they graduated you yet?"

"No. They're still working on it."

A waiter came by, deposited a napkin and a drink before him, took his money, glanced at the photos, gave me a wink and moved back toward the bar.

"I thought I had you cornered in History when I left," he said, raising the drink, taking a sip, pursing his lips, taking another. "What happened?"

"I escaped into Archaeology."

"Shaky. You had too many of the Anthro and Ancient History requirements for that to last long."

"True. But it provided a resting place for the second semester, which was all I needed. In the fall they started a Geology program. I mined that for a year and a half. By then, several new areas had opened up."

He shook his head.

"Exceptionally absurd," he said.

"Thank you."

I took a big, cold swallow.

He cleared his throat.

"How serious is this situation, anyway?"

"Offhand, I'd say it's fairly serious—though it seems to be based on a misunderstanding."

"I mean, does it involve the authorities—or private individuals?"

"Both, it seems. Why? You having second thoughts about helping me?"

"No, of course not! I was trying to estimate the opposition."

"I'm sorry," I said. "I guess I do owe you an appraisal of the risk . . ."

He raised a hand as if to stop me, but I went on anyway.

"I have no idea who that is outside. But at least a couple people involved in the whole business seem to be dangerous."

"All right, that is sufficient," he said. "I am, as always, totally responsible for my own actions, and I choose to assist you. Enough!"

We drank on it. He rearranged the pictures, smiling.

"I really *could* fix you up for tonight with one of them," he said, "if you wanted."

"Thanks. But tonight's my night for getting drunk."

"They are not mutually exclusive pastimes."

"They are tonight."

"Well," he said, shrugging, "I'd no intention to force anything on you. It is just that you aroused my hospitality. Success often does that."

"Success?"

"You are one of the few successful persons I know."

"Me? Why?"

"You know precisely what you are doing and you do it well."

"But I don't really do much of anything."

"And of course the quantity means nothing to you, nor the weight others place upon your actions. In my eyes, that makes you a success."

"By not giving a damn? But I do, you know."

"Of course you do, of course you do! But it is a matter of style, an awareness of choice—"

"Okay," I said. "Observation acknowledged and accepted in the proper spirit. Now—"

"—and that makes us kindred souls," he went on. "For I am just that way myself."

"Naturally. I knew it all along. Now about getting me out of here . . ."

"There is a kitchen with a back door to it," he said. "They serve meals here during the day. We will go out that way. The barman is a friend of mine. No problem there. Then I will take you a roundabout way to my place. There is a party should be going on there now. Enjoy as much as you want of it and sleep wherever you find a warm corner."

"Sounds very inviting, especially the corner. Thanks."

We finished our drinks and he put the ladies back in his pocket. He went to talk with the bartender and I saw the man nodding. Then he turned and gestured with his eyes toward the rear. I met him at the door to the kitchen.

He guided me through the kitchen and out the back door into an alleyway. I turned up my collar against the continuing drizzle and followed him off to the right. We turned left at an intersecting alley, passed among the dark shapes of trash containers, splashed through a lake of a puddle that soaked my socks and emerged near the middle of the next block.

Three or four blocks and twice as many minutes later, I followed him up the stairs in the building that held his quarters. The dampness had raised a musty smell and the stairs creaked beneath us. As we ascended, I heard faint sounds of music mixed in with voices and a bit of laughter.

We followed the sounds, coming at last to his door. We entered, he performed a dozen or so introductions and took my coat. I found a glass and some ice and some mix, took it and myself and my bottle to a chair and sat down, to talk, watch and hope that enjoyment was contagious while I drank myself into the big blank place that was waiting somewhere for me.

I found it eventually, of course, but not before seeing the party through to the dust-and-ashes stage. As everyone else present was headed along paths that led in the same direction, I did not feel too far removed from the action. Through the haze, the sound, the booze, everything came to seem normal, appropriate and unusually bright, even the re-entrance of Merimee, clad only in a garland of bay leaves and mounted on the small gray donkey that made its home in one of the back rooms. A grinning dwarf preceded him with a pair of cymbals. For a while, nobody seemed to notice. The procession halted before me.

"Fred?"

"Yes?"

"Before I forget, if you should oversleep in the morning and I'm gone when you get up, the bacon is in the lower drawer on the right in the refrigerator, and I keep the bread in the cupboard to the left. The eggs are in plain sight. Help yourself."

"Thanks. I'll remember that."

"One other thing . . ."

He leaned forward and lowered his voice.

"I've been doing a lot of thinking," he said.

"Oh?"

"About this trouble in which you find yourself?"

"Yeah?"

"I do not know quite how to put it . . . But . . . Do you think it possible you could be killed as a result?"

"I believe so."

"Well—only if it grows extremely pressing, mind you—but I have some acquaintances of a semisavory sort. If . . . If it becomes necessary for your own welfare that some individual predecease you, I would like you to have my phone number committed to memory. Call if you must, identify him and

93

mention where he can be found. I am owed a few favors. That can be one."

"I . . . I don't really know what to say. Thank you, of course. I hope I don't have to take you up on it. I never expected—"

"It is the least I could do to protect your Uncle Albert's investment."

"You knew of my Uncle Albert? Of his will? You never mentioned—"

"Knew of him? Al and I were schoolmates at the Sorbonne. Summers we used to run arms to Africa and points east. I blew my money. He hung onto his and made more. A bit of a poet, a bit of a scoundrel. It seems to run in your family. Classical mad Irishmen, all of you. Oh yes, I knew Al."

"Why didn't you mention this years ago?"

"You would have thought I was just pulling it on you to get you to graduate. That would not have been fair—interfering with your choices. Now, though, your present problems override my reticence."

"But—"

"Enough!" he said. "Let there be revelry!"

The dwarf banged the cymbals mightily, and Merimee extended his hand. Someone placed a bottle of wine in it. He threw back his head and drew a long, deep swig. The donkey began to prance. A sleepy-eyed girl seated near the hanging beads suddenly sprang to her feet, tearing at her hair and blouse buttons, crying, "Evoe! Evoe!" the while.

"See you around, Fred."

"Cheers."

At least, that is sort of how I remember it. Oblivion had crept perceptibly nearer by then, was almost touching my collar. I leaned back and let it go to work.

Sleep, that unwrinkleth the drip-dry garment of concern, found me later at that dust-and-ashes place where the people go out one by one. I made it to the mattress in the corner, sprawled there and said good night to the ceiling.

Then—

With the water streaming in the basin, lather on my face, Merimee's razor in my hand and me in the mirror, the mists fell away and there was Mt. Fuji. From this station, couched in the center of my most recent dark space, was the thing I had sought, freed by whatever arcane cue had just occurred:

DO
YOU
HEAR
ME, FRED?

YES.

GOOD.
THE UNIT
IS PROPERLY
PROGRAMMED
OUR PURPOSES
WILL BE SERVED.

WHAT ARE
OUR PURPOSES?

A SINGLE
TRANSFORMATION
IS ALL THAT WILL
BE NECESSARY NOW.

WHAT SORT OF
TRANSFORMATION?

PASSAGE
THROUGH THE
MOBILATOR OF THE
N-AXIAL INVERSION UNIT.

YOU
MEAN THE
CENTRAL COMPONENT
OF THE RHENNIUS
MACHINE?

AFFIRMATIVE.

WHAT DO YOU
WANT ME TO
RUN THROUGH IT?

YOURSELF.

MYSELF?
YOURSELF.

WHY?

VITAL
TRANSFORMATION.

OF WHAT SORT?

INVERSION,
OF COURSE.
WHY INVERT?

NECESSARY.
IT WILL SET
EVERYTHING IN
PROPER ORDER.

BY REVERSING ME?

EXACTLY.

COULD IT
BE DANGEROUS
TO MY HEALTH?

NO
MORE
THAN MANY
OTHER THINGS
YOU DO IN THE COURSE
OF YOUR DAILY AFFAIRS.

WHAT
ASSURANCE
HAVE I OF THIS?

MINE.

IF I RECALL
CORRECTLY, YOU ARE A
RECORDING.

I—XXXX
XXXXXXXXX

```
        XXXXXXXXXX
        XXXX I—XX
        XXXXXXXXXXX
        XXXXXXXXX I—
        XXXSPEICUSPEIC
        USPEICUSPEICUSP
        EICUSXXXXXXXXXXX
        PEICXXXUSPEIXXXXX
        XXXXXXXXXXXXXXXX
```

NEVER MIND.

```
XXXXXXXXXXXXXXXXXX
XXXXXXXXXXXXXXXXXX
DO YOU HEAR ME, FRED?
DO YOU HEAR ME, FRED?
```

STILL HERE.

WILL YOU DO IT?

JUST ONCE
THROUGH THE THING?

CORRECT.
BY NO MEANS
MORE THAN THAT.

WHY NOT?
WHAT WOULD
HAPPEN IF I
REPEATED IT?

I AM
HAMPERED
BY THE LACK
OF AN ALGEBRAIC
SOLUTION TO A GENERAL
EQUATION OF THE FIFTH
DEGREE.

JUST TELL ME
IN PLAIN WORDS.

IT WOULD
BE DANGEROUS
TO YOUR HEALTH.

HOW DANGEROUS?

TERMINALLY SO.

I AM
NOT CERTAIN
I LIKE THE IDEA.

NECESSARY.
IT WILL SET
EVERYTHING IN
PROPER ORDER.

YOU ARE SURE THAT
IT WILL HAVE THE EFFECT
OF MAKING THINGS
CLEARER,

OF BRINGING SOME
ORDER
TO
THE PRESENT MUDDLED
SITUATION?

OH YESXXXXX
XXYESXXYESXX
YESYESYESYES
YESYESYESYES
YESYESYESYES
XXXXXXXXYES.

I AM
GLAD
YOU ARE SO
CONFIDENT.

THEN YOU
WILL DO IT?

IT IS
SUFFICIENTLY
BIZARRE TO BE
A HAIR OF THE DOG.

PLEASE CLARIFY.
YES.
AFFIRMATIVE.
I WILL DO IT.

YOU WILL NOT
HAVE REGRETS.

                    LET
                    US HOPE.
                    WHEN SHOULD
                    I BE ABOUT IT?

            AS SOON
        AS POSSIBLE.

                    ALL RIGHT
                    I WILL THINK
                    OF SOME WAY TO
                    GET AT IT AGAIN.

            THAT
            THEN
                IS ALLOOOOOOOOOOOOOOOO
OOOOOOOOOOOOOOOOOOOOOOOOOOOOOOOOOOOO
OOOOOOOOOOOOOOOOOOOOOOOOOOOOOOOOOOOO
OOOOOOOOOOOOOOOOOOOOOOOOOOOOOOOOOO

There it was, in its entirety. Instant replay—only in less time
than it took me to raise my hand to my cheek and cut a highway
through the lather. My nameless respondent had come through
all right, and this time he had promised a satisfying result. I began to hum. Even a shaky assurance of enlightenment is better
than indefinite uncertainty.

When I had finished, I bypassed the front room and made
my way into the kitchen. It was a narrow place, with a sink
full of dirty dishes and the smell of curry in the air. I set about
assembling a meal.

In the lower right-hand drawer of the refrigerator, lying atop
the package of bacon, I discovered a note. It said simply: "Remember the number and what I said about calling it."

So I ran the digits through my mind, over and over, as I scrambled, fried and toasted. Then, just as I was sitting down to eat, the donkey came into the kitchen and stared at me.

"Coffee?" I suggested.

"Stop that!"

"What?"

"Those numbers. It is extremely irritating."

"What numbers?"

"The ones you are thinking. They are swarming like insects."

I spread marmalade on a piece of toast and took a bite.

"Go to hell," I said. "My uses for telepathic donkeys are limited, and what I do in the privacy of my own mind is my business."

"The human mind, Mister Cassidy, is seldom worth the visit. I assure you I did not request the assignment of monitoring yours. It is obvious now that I erred in mentioning a creature courtesy you cannot appreciate. I suppose that I should apologize."

"Go ahead."

"You go to hell."

I started in on the eggs and bacon. A minute or two passed.

"My name is Sibla," the donkey said.

I decided that I did not really care and went on eating.

"I am a friend of Ragma—and Charv."

"I see," I said, "and they sent you to spy on me, to poke around in my mind."

"That is not so. I was assigned the job of protecting you until you were fit to receive a message and act on it."

"How were you to protect me?"

"By keeping you inconspicuous—"

"With a donkey following me around? Who briefed you, anyway?"

"I am aware of my prominence in this guise. I was about to explain that my task was to provide for your mental silence. As a telepath, I am capable of dampening your thought noises. It has not really been necessary, however, in that alcohol deadens them considerably. Still, I am here to shield you against premature betrayal of your position to another telepath."

"What other telepath?"

"To be more honest than may be necessary, I do not know. It was decided at some level other than my own that there might be a telepath involved in this case. I was sent here both to keep you silent and to block any unfriendly telepath trying to reach you. Also, I was to attempt to determine the identity and whereabouts of that individual."

"Well? What happened?"

"Nothing. You were drunk and no one tried to reach you."

"So the guess was wrong."

"Possibly. Possibly not."

I resumed eating. Between mouthfuls, I asked, "What is your level or rank, or whatever? The same as Charv's and Ragma's? Or are you higher up?"

"Neither," the donkey replied. "I am in budget analysis and cost accounting. I was drafted as the only available telepath capable of assuming this role."

"Are you under any restrictions as to what you can tell me?"

"I was told to exercise my judgment and common sense."

"Strange. Nothing else about this business seems particularly rational. They must not have had time to brief you fully."

"True. There was quite a rush about it. I had to allow for travel time and the substitution."

"What substitution?"

"The real donkey is tied up out back."

"Uh-huh."

"I am reading your thoughts, and I am not about to give you any answers Ragma refused you."

"Okay. If your common sense and good judgment tell you to withhold information that may be vital to my safety, then by all means be sensible." I swallowed the final forkful. "What's that message you mentioned?"

The donkey looked away.

"You had expressed some willingness to cooperate in the investigation, had you not?"

"I had—earlier," I said.

"You would not agree to go offworld to be examined by a telepathic analyst, however."

"That is correct."

"We were wondering whether you might be willing to allow me to attempt it—here, now."

I took a sip of coffee.

"Have you had much training along these lines?"

"Just about every telepath knows something of the theory involved, and of course I possess a lifetime of experience with telepathy—"

"You are a cost accountant," I said. "Don't try to impress the natives."

"All right. I am not trained for it. I think I can do it, though. So do the others, or I would not have been approached to try."

"Who are the others?"

"Well . . . Oh hell! Charv and Ragma."

"I've a feeling they are not proceeding according to the manual in this. Correct?"

"Field agents in their line of work possess a great deal of discretionary authority. They have to."

I sighed and lit a cigarette.

"How old is the organization which employs you?" I said. When I detected hesitation, I added, "Surely there is no harm in telling me that."

"I guess not. Several thousand—years, by your measure."

"I see. In other words, it is one of the biggest, oldest bureacracies around."

"I see in your mind what you are getting at, but—"

"Let me shape it anyway. As a student of business administration, I know that there is a law of evolution for organizations as stringent and inevitable as anything in life. The longer one exists, the more it grinds out restrictions that slow its own functions. It reaches entropy in a state of total narcissism. Only the people sufficiently far out in the field get anything done, and every time they do they are breaking half a dozen rules in the process."

"I will grant you that that view is not without some merit. But in our case—"

"Your proposal violates some rule. I know it. I do not have to read your mind to know that you are uneasy about this whole affair because of it. Isn't that right?"

"I am not permitted to discuss policies and internal operating procedures."

"Naturally," I said, "but I had to say it. Now tell me about this analysis business. How do you go about it?"

"It would be similar to the simple word association test with which you are familiar. The difference is that I will do it from the inside. I will not have to guess at your reactions. I will know them at a primary level."

"This seems to indicate that you cannot look directly into my subconscious."

"That is correct. I am not that good. Ordinarily, I can only read your surface thoughts. When I hit something this way, though, I should be able to keep pressing the feeling and follow it on down to where its roots are twisted."

"I see. Then it does require considerable cooperation on my part?"

"Oh yes. It would take a real pro to push in against your will."

"I guess I am fortunate there are none of them available."

"I wish there were. I am certain that I am not going to enjoy it."

I finished my coffee and poured another cup.

"What do you say to our doing it this afternoon?" Sibla asked.

"What's wrong with right now?"

"I would rather wait for your nervous system to return to normal. There are still some secondary effects from the beverages you consumed. They make scanning you more difficult."

"Does that always hold?"

"By and large."

"Interesting."

I sipped more coffee.

"You are doing it again!"

"What?"

"Those numbers, over and over."

"Sorry. Hard to keep them out."

"That is *not* the reason!"

I stood. I stretched.

"Excuse me. I require the use of the facility again."

Sibla moved to block my way, but I moved faster.

"You are not thinking of leaving, are you? Is that what you are masking?"

"I never said that."

"You do not have to. I can feel it. You will be making a mistake if you do."

I headed for the door, and Sibla turned quickly to follow.

"I will not permit you to go—not after the indignities I have suffered to get at that miserable knot of ganglia!"

"That's a nice way to talk!" I said. "Especially when you want a favor."

I dashed up the hall and into the john. Sibla clattered after.

"We are doing you the favor! Only you are too stupid to realize it!"

" 'Uninformed' is the word—and that's your fault!"

I slammed the door, locked it.

"Wait! Listen! If you go, you could be in real trouble!"

I laughed. "I'm sorry. You came on too strong."

I turned to the window, flung it wide.

"Then go, you ignorant ape! Throw away your chance at civilization!"

"What are you talking about?"

Silence.

Then: "Nothing. I am sorry. But you must realize that it is important."

"I already know that. What I want to know is 'Why?' "

"I cannot tell you."

"Then go to hell," I said.

"I knew you were not worth it," Sibla replied. "From what I have seen of your race, you are nothing but a band of barbarians and degenerates."

I swung up onto the sill, crouched a moment while I estimated the distance.

"Nobody likes a smartass either," I said, and then I jumped.

7

DENNIS WEXROTH DIDN'T say a damn thing. If he had, I might have killed him just then. He stood there with his palms pressed against the wall behind him; a deepening redness about his right eyesocket where it would eventually puff up and go purple. The receiver of his uprooted telephone hung over the edge of the wastebasket where I had hurled it.

In my hand was a fancy piece of parchment which told me that Frederick Cunningham Cassidy had received a Philosophy of Doctorate in Anthropology.

Fighting for some measure of control, I slipped it back into its envelope and dammed my river of profanity.

"How?" I said. "How could you possibly do such a thing? It . . . It's illegal!"

"It is perfectly legal," he said softly. "Believe me, it was done under advice."

"We'll just see how that advice holds up in court," I said. "I was never admitted to grad school, I haven't submitted a dissertation, I never took any orals or language exams and no notice was filed. Now you tell me how you justify giving me a Ph.D. I'd really like to know."

"First, you are enrolled here," he said. "That makes you eligible for a degree."

"Eligible, yes. Entitled, no. There *is* a distinction."

"True, but the elements of entitlement are determined by the administration."

"What did you do? Have a special meeting?"

"As a matter of fact, there was one. And it was determined that enrollment as a full-time student was to be deemed indicative of the intention to take a degree. Consequently, if the other factors were met—"

"I've never completed a major," I said.

"The formal course requirements are less rigid when it comes to the matter of an advanced degree."

"But I never took a B.A.!"

He smiled, thought better of it, erased it.

"If you will read the regulations very carefully," he said, "you will see that nowhere do they state that a baccalaureate is a prerequisite for an advanced degree. A 'suitable equivalent' is sufficient to produce a 'qualified candidate.' They are phrases of art, Fred, and the administration does the construing."

"Even granting that, the dissertation requirement *is* written into the regs. I've read that part."

"Yes. But then there is *Sacred Ground: A Study of Ritual Areas,* the book you submitted to the university press. It is sufficiently appropriate to warrant treatment as an anthropology dissertation."

"I've never submitted it to the department for anything."

"No, but the editor asked Dr. Lawrence's opinion of it. His opinion, among other things, was that it would do for a dissertation."

"I'll nail you on that point when I get you in court," I said. "But go on. I'm fascinated. Tell me how I did on my orals."

"Well," he said, looking away, "the professors who would have sat on your board agreed unanimously to waive the orals in your case. You have been around so long and they know you so well that they considered it an unnecessary formality. Besides, two of them were classmates of yours as undergraduates and they felt kind of funny about it."

"I'll bet they did. Let me finish the story myself. The heads of the language departments involved decided I had taken sufficient courses in their respective bailiwicks to warrant their certifying as to my reading abilities. Right?"

"That, basically, is it."

"It was easier to give me a doctorate than a B.A.?"

"Yes, it was."

I wanted to hit him again, but that wasn't the answer. I drove my fist into my palm, several times.

"Why?" I said. "Now I know how you did it, but the really important thing is why." I began to pace. "I've paid this university its tuitions, its fees, for some thirteen years now—a decent little sum when you stop to add things up—and I've never bounced a check here, or anything like that. I have always gotten along well with the faculty, the administration, the other students. Except for my climbing, I've never been in any really serious trouble, done anything to give the place a black eye . . . Pardon me. What I am trying to say is that I've been a pretty decent customer for what you are selling. Then what happens? I turn my back, I go out of town for a little while and you slip me a Ph.D. Do I deserve that kind of treatment after giving you my patronage all this time? I think it was a rotten thing to do and I want an explanation. Now, I want one. Now! Do you really hate me that much?"

"Feelings had nothing to do with it," he said, raising his hand slowly to prod the upper reaches of his cheek. "I told you I wanted to get you out of here because I did not approve of your attitude, your style. That still holds. But this was none of

110

my doing. In fact, I opposed it. There were—well—pressures brought to bear on us."

"What kind of pressures?" I asked.

He turned away. "I do not believe I am the one to be talking about it, really."

"You are," I said. "Really. Tell me about it."

"Well, the university gets a lot of money from the government, you know. Grants, research contracts . . ."

"I know. What of it?"

"Ordinarily, they keep their nose out of our business."

"Which is as it should be."

"Occasionally, though, they have something to say. When they do, we generally listen."

"Are you trying to tell me I've been awarded my degree by government request?"

"In a word, yes."

"I don't believe you. They just don't do things like that."

He shrugged. Then he turned and looked at me again.

"There was a time when I would have said the same thing," he told me, "but I know better now."

"Why did they want it done?"

"I still have no idea."

"I find that difficult to believe."

"I was told that the reason for the request was of a confidential nature. I was also told that it was a matter of some urgency, and he waved the word 'security' at us. That was all that I was told."

I stopped pacing. I jammed my hands into my pockets. I took them out again. I found a cigarette and lit it. It tasted funny. But then, they all did these days. Everything did.

"A man named Nadler," he said, "Theodore Nadler. He is with the State Department. He is the one who contacted us and suggested . . . the arrangements."

"I see," I said. "Is that who you were trying to call when I removed the means of doing it?"

"Yes."

He glanced at his desk, crossed to it, picked up his pipe and his pouch.

"Yes," he repeated, loading the bowl. "He asked me to get in touch with him if I caught sight of you. Since you have seen to it that I can't do it right now, I would suggest that you call him yourself if you want further particulars."

He put the pipe between his teeth, leaned forward and scrawled a number on a pad. He tore the sheet off and handed it to me.

I took it, glanced at the screwed-up digits, stuck it into my pocket. Wexroth lit his pipe.

"And you really don't know what he wants of me?" I said.

He pushed his chair back into its proper position, then seated himself.

"I have no idea."

"Well," I said, "I feel better for having hit you, anyway. I'll see you in court."

I turned to go.

"I do not believe anyone has ever sought an order directing a university to rescind his degree," he said. "It should be interesting. In the meantime, I cannot say that I am unhappy to see an end to your drone- hood."

"Save the celebration," I said. "I haven't finished yet."

"You and the Flying Dutchman," he muttered just before I slammed the door.

I had descended into an alleyway, up the block and around the corner from Merimee's place. Minutes later I was in a taxi and headed uptown. I got out at a clothing store, went in and bought a coat. It was chilly and I had left my jacket behind. From there, I walked to the hall. I had plenty of time and I wanted to determine, if possible, whether I was being followed.

I spent almost an hour in that big room where they kept the Rhennius machine. I wondered whether my other visit there had made the morning news. No matter. I paid attention to the movements of the viewers, to the positions of the four guards—there had only been two before—to the distances to the several entrances, to everything. I could not tell whether a new grille was yet in place on the other side of one of the overhead windows. Not that it really mattered. I had no intention of trying the same trick a second time. I was after something fast and different.

Musing, I went out to locate a sandwich and a beer, the latter for the benefit of any telepaths in the neighborhood. While I was about it, I kept checking and decided that I was not, at the moment, the subject of conspicuous scrutiny. I found a place, entered, ordered, settled down to eating and thought.

The idea hit me at the same time as a blast of cold air let in by a prospective diner. I rejected it immediately and continued with my beef and brew. But I could not come up with anything better.

So I resurrected it, cleaned it up and looked at it from every angle I could think of. Not much of an inspiration, but I was afraid it would have to do.

I figured the whole thing out, then realized that it might not work because of a side effect of the process itself. I beat back a moment's frustration, then started in again, at the beginning. It wobbled on the brink of the ridiculous, the little things I had to cover because of something so minor.

I journeyed to the bus station and purchased a ticket home. I put it in my coat pocket. I bought a magazine and some chewing gum, had them put in a bag, disposed of the magazine, chewed the gum, kept the bag. Then I went look-ing for a bank, found one, went in and changed all my mon-ey into one-dollar bills, which I stuffed into the bag—one hundred fifteen in all.

Making my way back to the neighborhood of the hall, I searched out a restaurant with a coat-checking operation, left my coat and slipped back outside again. I used the wad of chew-ing gum to affix the coat receipt to the underside of a bench on which I sat for a while. Then I smoked a final cigarette and headed back for the hall, the bag of money in one hand, a single dollar bill palmed in the other.

Inside, I moved slowly, waiting for the crowd to achieve the proper density and distribution, rechecking my remembrance of air drafts on the opening and closing of the outer doors. I decided on the best position for the enterprise and worked my way toward it. By that time I had torn the bag down one side and was holding it together.

Around five minutes later the situation struck me as being about as close to ideal as it was likely to get. The crowd was effectively dense and the guards sufficiently distant. I listened to the by then standard "But what does it *do?*" and "They're not really certain," with an occasional "It's some kind of re-versing thing. They're studying it" thrown in, until there was both a sharp draft and an appropriately large individual near-by.

I gave the guy an elbow in the ribs and a bit of a push. He, in turn, gave me a sample of Middle English—most people seem to think it is an Anglo-Saxonism, but I once looked it up in connection with a linguistics course—and he returned my shove.

I exaggerated my reaction, staggering back and bumping into another man while seeing to it that the bag came apart with a grand flourish high above my head.

"My money!" I screamed, springing forward then and leaping the guardrail. "My money!"

I ignored the murmurs, the shouts and the sudden scrambling that occurred behind me. I had triggered the alarm also, but the fact was not especially material at the moment. I was onto the platform and racing about it toward the place where the belt entered the central unit. I hoped that it was able to bear my weight.

I countered a bellowed "Get down from there!" with a couple of repetitions of "My money!" as I threw myself flat on the belt with what I hoped appeared a good dollar-chasing gesture, and I was borne surely and smoothly into the tunnel of the mobilator.

A tiny tingling sensation swept me from head to foot as I passed through the thing, and I experienced a momentary blurring of vision. This did not prevent my unfolding the dollar I had palmed, however, so that I emerged clenching it on high. I immediately rolled from the belt and, despite a wave of dizziness, jumped down from the platform and rushed back toward the crowd, trying to seem as if I still pursued my errant money, though none was then in sight.

"My money . . ." I said as I climbed back over the rail and dropped to all fours.

"Here's some," an honest soul remarked, thrusting a fistful of bills down before my face.

ƎNO by ƎNO, a number of others were handed to me. Fortunately, the anticipation of this effect had been part of my earlier meditations, so that my reversed face showed no signs of surprise as I rose and thanked them. The only bill that looked normal to me was the one I had carried in my hand.

"Did you go through that thing?" a man asked.

"No. I went around behind it."

"Sure looked like you went through."

"No. I didn't."

As I accepted money and pretended to look for more, I did a rapid scan of the entire hall. The less honest folks with a few of my dollars in their pockets were heading out the doors, which were now in positions opposite those they had occupied when I had entered. But for this, too, had I prepared myself—at least intellectually. Now, though, I wondered. It was emotionally disconcerting, seeing the whole hall in reverse like that. And those departing were getting out without difficulty, for the guards were otherwise occupied: two were stuck in the crowd and two were collecting bills. I debated making a run for it.

At first, I had been all set to brazen it out with the guards or anyone else involved, matching nastiness or officiousness with a greater obnoxiousness over my missing money and an insistence that I had gone around rather than through the device. I had decided that I could stick to that format and sit out any consequences. After all, I did not believe that I had done anything grossly illegal—and no matter what happened, they could not take back the reversal.

Instead, they were nice about it. One of them got the alarm shut off and another shouted at everyone to turn in any money they had recovered as they departed the hall. Then two of them moved to cover the doors again, and the one who had done the hollering sought me with his eyes, found me and raised his voice once more: "Are you all right?"

"Yes," I said. "I'm all right. But my money—"

"We're getting it! We're getting it!"

He plowed his way through to my side, laid his hand on my shoulder. I hastily pocketed the one bill that looked normal to me.

"Are you sure you're okay?"

"Of course. But I'm missing—"

"We are trying to recover it," he said. "Did you go through the center part of that machine?"

"No," I said. "A bill blew past it, though, and I chased it."

"It looked like you went through the center unit."

"He went around behind it," said one of the men I had told that to, as neatly timed as if he had been sitting on my knee with a monocle in one eye, bless him.

"Yes," I said.

"Oh. You didn't get any shocks or anything like that, did you?"

"No, but I got my dollar."

"That's good." He sighed. "Glad we don't have to fill out an accident report. What happened, anyway?"

"A guy bumped me and my bag tore. I had the morning's receipts in it. My boss will take it out of my pay if—"

"Let's go see how much has been collected."

We did, and I got back ninety-seven dollars, almost enough to let me think a good thought about my fellow man and throw in a brass button for providence for having run a very tight ship so far that day. I left a phony name and address for them to contact, should any other bills turn up, thanked them several times, apologized for the disturbance and got out.

Traffic, I noticed immediately, was proceeding up and down the wrong sides of the street. Okay, I could live with that. The signs in store windows were all backward. Okay. That, too.

I started out for the bench where I had stashed my coat receipt. I drew up short after a dozen paces.

It had to be the wrong direction, because it felt right.

I stood there then and tried to visualize the whole city as reversed. It was more difficult than I had thought it would be. My roast beef and beer—now reversed—churned in my innards, and I wanted to grab hold of something and hang on. I fought everything back into place, or what seemed like place, and turned. Yes. Better. The trick was to navigate by landmarks and pretend I was shaving. Think of it all as in a mirror. I wondered whether a dentist would have an advantage at something like this, or if his ability only extended to the insides of mouths. No matter. I had figured out where the bench was.

I got to it, panicked when I could not locate the receipt, then remembered to go over to the opposite end. Yes. Right there . . .

I had, of course, planted the receipt so that it would not be reversed and cause me difficulty in getting my coat back. And I had checked the coat so the ticket would not be reversed, causing me difficulty in boarding my bus.

I mapped out the route image in my mind and found my way back to the restaurant. I was prepared for its situation on the opposite side of the street but still fumbled the door by reaching to the wrong side for its handle.

The girl fetched me my coat promptly, but "It ain't April Fool's Day," she said as I turned to leave.

"Huh?"

She waved a bill at me. Lacking change, I had decided to leave a dollar tip. I realized at that moment that I had pulled out my one normal-looking bill, the dollar I had carried through the mobilator.

"Oh," I said and added a quick grin. "That was for the party. Here, I'll trade you."

I gave her a ƎИO for it and she decided she could smile, too.

"It felt real," she said. "I couldn't tell what was wrong with it for a second."

"Yeah. Great gag."

I stopped to buy a pack of cigarettes, then headed off to relocate the bus station. In that I still had plenty of time before departure, I decided that a little more antitelepath medicine might be in order. I entered an undistinguished-looking bar and got me a mug of beer.

It tasted strange. Not bad. Just very different. I backspelled the name on the tap and asked the bartender if that was what was really under it. He said that it was. I shrugged and sipped it. It was actually pretty good. Then the cigarette that I lit tasted peculiar. At first, I attributed this to the aftertaste of the beer. A few moments later, though, a half-formed thought caused me to call the bartender back again and have him pour me a shot of bourbon.

It had a rich, smoky taste, unlike anything I had ever had out of a bottle bearing that label. Or any other label, for that matter.

Then some recollections from Organic Chem I and II were suddenly with me. All of my amino acids, with the exception of glycine, had been left-handed, accounting for the handedness of my protein helices. Ditto for the nucleotides, giving that twisting to the coils of nucleic acid. But that was before my reversal. I thought madly about stereoisomers and nutrition. It seemed that the body sometimes accepted substances of one handedness and rejected the reversed version of the same thing. Then, in other cases, it would accept both, though digestion would take longer in the one case than the other. I tried to recall specific cases. My beer and the shot contained ethyl alcohol, C_2H_5OH . . . Okay. It was symmetrical, with the two hydrogen atoms coming off the central carbon atom that way. Reversed or unreversed, then, I would get just as stoned on it. Then why did it taste different? The congeners, yes. They were asymmetrical esters and they tickled my taste buds in a different way. My olfactory apparatus had to be playing backward games with the cigarette smoke also. I realized that I would have to look some things up in a hurry when I got home. Since I did not know how long I would be a *Spiegelmensch*, I wanted to provide against malnutrition, if this were a real danger.

I finished the beer. I would have a long bus ride during which I could consider the phenomenon in more detail. In the meantime, it seemed prudent to dodge around a bit and make certain whether or not I was being followed again. I went out and did this for the next fifteen or twenty minutes, but was unable to detect anyone trailing me. I moved on to the station, then, to catch my stereoisobus back home.

Drifting drowsy across the countryside, I paraded my troubles through the streets of my mind, poking occasional thoughts between the bars of their cages, hearing the clowns beat drums in my temples, I had performed my assigned task. Assigned by whom? Well, he had said he was a recording, but he had also furnished me with Article 7224, Section C, in a time of need—and anyone who helps me when I need help is automatically on the side of the angels until further notice. I wondered whether I was supposed to get drunk again for additional instructions or whether he had something else in mind for our next contact. There had to be one, of course. He had indicated that my cooperation on this venture would lead to all manner of clarification and untanglement. All right. I bought it. I was willing to take, on faith in that promise, the necessity for my reversal. Everyone else had wanted something I could not provide and offered nothing in return.

If I drifted off to sleep, would there be another message? Or was my alcohol level too low? And what was the connection there, anyway? If Sibla was to be believed, alcohol acted as a dampener rather than an exciter of telepathic phenomena. Why had my correspondent come through most clearly on the two occasions when I had been intoxicated? It occurred to me at that moment that if it were not for the obvious effect of Article 7224, Section C, I would have no way of really knowing that the communications were not simply drunken hallucinations, perhaps the best efforts to date of a highly imaginative death wish. But it had to be more than that. Even Charv and Ragma now suspected the existence of my supersensory accomplice. I felt a sense of urgency, a need to do whatever had to be done quickly, before the aliens caught on to the pattern—whatever it might be. I was certain that they would disapprove, probably attempt to interfere.

How many of them were there, pursuing or watching me? Where were Zeemeister and Buckler? What were Charv and Ragma up to? Who was the man in the dark coat Merimee had spotted? What was the State Department representative doing? Since I had answers for none of these questions, I devoted some time to planning my own actions so as to allow for the worst of everything. I would not go back to my apartment, for obvious reasons. Hal's place seemed a bit risky, with all the activity he had described. I decided that Ralph Warp ought to be able to put me up for a time in an appropriately surreptitious fashion. After all, I owned half of the Woof & Warp, his arts-and-crafts shop, and had sacked out in the back room in the past. Yes, that was what I would do.

Steinway-like, the ghost of exertions past fell upon me then, as from a great height, and I was crumpled. Hoping for further enlightenment, I did not fight the crush. But drowsing there in my seat, I was not rewarded with another message. Instead, a nightmare encompassed me.

I dreamed I was staked out in the blazing sun once more, sweating, burning, achieving raisinhood. This reached a hellish peak, then shifted away, faded. I rediscovered myself stranded on an iceberg, teeth chattering, extremities growing numb. Then this, too, passed, but wave after wave of muscular tics swept me from toe to crown. Then I was afraid. Then angry. Elated. Horny. Despairing. With naked feet stalking, the full parade of feelings passed, clad in forms that flee from me. It was no dream . . .

"Mister, are you all right?"

There was a hand on my shoulder—from that dream or this?

"Are you all right?"

I shuddered. I rubbed a hand across my forehead. It came away wet.

"Yes," I said. "Thanks."

I glanced at the man. Elderly. Neatly dressed. Off to see the grandchildren, perhaps.

"I was sitting across the aisle," he said. "Looked like you were having some sort of fit."

I rubbed my eyes, ran my hand through my hair, touched my chin and discovered I had been drooling.

"Bad dream," I said. "I'm okay now. Thanks for waking me up."

He gave me a small smile, nodded and withdrew.

Damn! It just seemed to follow that it had to be some side effect of the reversal. I lit a funny-tasting cigarette and glanced at my watch. After deciphering the reversed dial and allowing for its being wrong anyway, I decided I had been dozing for about half an hour. Staring out the window, then, watching the miles pass, I grew quite afraid. What if the whole thing were a ghastly joke, a mistake or a misunderstanding? The little episode that had just occurred left me with the fear that I had screwed myself up inside at some level I had not yet considered, that subtle, irreversible damages might be taking place within me. Kind of late to think of that, though. I made an effort to maintain my faith in my friend, the recording. I felt certain that the Rhennius machine could undo what it had done when this became necessary. All that was required was someone who understood how it worked.

I sat for a long while, hoping for some answer to come. The only thing that arrived, however, was more drowsiness and eventual sleep. This time it was the big, dark, quiet thing it is supposed to be, sans all vicissitudes and *angst,* peaceful. All the way through into night and my station, I slept. Refreshed for a change, I stepped down to familiar concrete, remapped the world about me and threaded my way through its parking lot, an alley and four blocks of closed stores.

I satisfied myself that I was not being followed, entered an all-night diner and ate a strange-tasting meal. Strange, because the place was a greasy spoon and the food was deliciously different. I ate two of their notorious hamburgers and great masses of soggy French fries. A sheaf of wilted lettuce and several slices of overripe tomato added to the treat. I wolfed everything down, not really caring whether or not it satisfied all my nutritional needs. It was the finest meal I had ever eaten. Except for the milkshake. It was undrinkable and I left it.

Then I walked. It was a good distance, but then. I was in no hurry, I was rested and my posterior had had enough of public transportation for a time. It took the better part of an hour to reach the Woof & Warp, but it was a good night for walking.

The shop was closed, of course, but I could see a light in Ralph's apartment upstairs. I went around back, shinnied up the drainpipe and peered in the window. He sat reading a book, and I could hear the faint sounds of a string quartet—I couldn't tell whose—from within. Good. That he was alone, I mean. I hate to break in on people.

I rapped on the pane.

He looked up, stared a moment, rose and came over.

The window slid upward.

"Hi, Fred. Come on in."

"Thanks, Ralph. How've you been?"

"Fine," he said. "Business has been good, too."

"Great."

I climbed in, closed the window, crossed the room with him. I accepted a drink whose taste I did not recognize, though it looked like a fruit juice there in the pitcher on the table. We sat down, and I did not feel especially disoriented. He rearranges his rooms so often that I can never remember the layout from one time to the next, anyway. Ralph is a tall, wiry guy with lots of dark hair and bad posture. He knows all manner of crafty things. Even teaches basket weaving at the university.

"How did you like Australia?"

"Oh, barring a few mishaps, I might have enjoyed it. I haven't decided yet."

"What sort of mishaps?"

"Later, later," I said. "Another time, maybe. Say, would it be too much trouble to put me up in the back room tonight?"

"Not unless you and Woof have had an argument."

"We have an arrangement," I said. "He sleeps with his nose under his tail and I get the blankets."

"The last time you stayed over it worked out the other way around."

"That's what led to the arrangement."

"We'll see what happens this time. Did you just get back in town?"

"Well, yes and no."

He clasped his hands about his knee and smiled.

"I admire your straightforward approach to things, Fred. Nothing evasive or misleading about you."

"I'm always being misunderstood," I said. "It is the burden of an honest man in a world of knaves. Yes, I just got back in town, but not from Australia. I did that a couple days ago, then went away and just now came back again. No, I did not just get back in town from Australia. See?"

He shook his head.

"You have a simple, almost classic lifestyle, too. What sort of trouble are you in this time? Irate husband? Mad bomber? Syndicate creditor?"

"Nothing like that," I said.

"Worse? Or better?"

"More complicated. What have you heard?"

"Nothing. But your adviser phoned me."

"When?"

"A little over a week ago. Then again this morning."

"What did he want?"

"He wanted to know where you were, wanted to know whether I had heard from you. I told him no on both counts. He told me a man would be stopping by to ask some questions. The university would appreciate my cooperation. That was the first time. The man showed up a little later, asked me the same questions, got the same answers."

"Was his name Nadler?"

"Yes. A federal man. State Department. At least, that is what his I.D. said. He gave me a number and told me to call it if I heard from you."

"Don't."

He winced.

"You didn't have to say it."

"Sorry."

I listened to the strings.

"I haven't heard from him since," he finished a few moments later.

"What did Wexroth want this morning?"

"He had the same questions, updated, and a message."

"For me?"

He nodded. He took a sip of his drink.

"What is it?"

"If I heard from you I was to tell you that you have graduated. You can pick up your diploma at his office."

"What?"

I was on my feet, part of my drink slopping over onto my cuff.

"That's what he said: 'graduated.' "

"They can't do that to me!"

He hunched his shoulders, let them fall again.

"Was he joking? Did he sound stoned? Did he say why? How?"

"No—on all of them," he said. "He sounded sober and serious. He even repeated it."

"Damn!" I began to pace. "Who do they think they are? You can't just force a degree on a man that way."

"Some people want them."

"They don't have frozen uncles. Damn! I wonder what happened? I don't see any angle. I've never given them an opening for this. How the hell could they do it?"

"I don't know. You'll have to ask him."

"I will! Believe me, I will! I'm going down there first thing in the morning and punch him in the eye!"

"Will that solve anything?"

"No, but revenge fits in with a classic life-style."

I sat down again and drank my drink. The music went round and round.

Later, after reminding the merry-eyed Irish Setter who worked as night watchman on the first floor that we had an arrangement involving tails and blankets, I sacked out on the bed in the back room. A dream of wondrous symbolism and profundity came to me there.

Many years earlier I had read an amusing little book called *Sphereland* by a mathematician named Burger. It was a sequel to the old Abbott classic *Flatland*, and in it there had been a bit of business involving the reversal of two-dimensional creatures by a being from higher space. Pedigreed dogs and mongrels were mirror images of one another, symmetrical but not congruent. The pedigreed mutts were rarer, more expensive, and a little girl had wanted one so badly. Her father arranged for her mongrel to be mated with a pedigreed dog, in hope that it would produce the more desirable pups. But alas, while there was a large litter, they were all of them mongrels. Later, however, an obliging visitor from higher space turned them into pedigreed dogs by rotating them through the third dimension. The geometric moral, while well taken, was not what had fascinated me about the incident, though. I kept trying to picture the mating that had taken place—two symmetrical but incongruent dogs going at it in two dimensions. The only available procedure involved a kind of *canis obversa* position, which I visualized and then imagined as rotating, whirligig-like, in two-dimensional space. I had employed the mandala thus achieved as a meditation aid in my yoga classes for some time afterward. Now it returned to me in the halls of slumber, and I was surrounded and crowded by pairs of deadly serious dogs, curling and engendering, doing their thing silently, spinning, occasionally nipping one another about the neck. Then an icy wind swept down upon me and the dogs vanished and I was cold and alone and afraid.

I awoke to discover that Woof had stolen the blankets and was sleeping on them off in the corner by the potting kiln. Snarling, I went over and recovered them. He tried to pretend it was all a misunderstanding, the son of a bitch, but I knew better and I told him so. When I glanced over later, all that I could see was his tail and a mournful expression among the dust and the potsherds.

8

THEY WERE WAITING FOR ME to say something, to do something. But there was nothing to say, nothing to do. We were going to die, and that was that. I glanced out the window and along the beach to the place where the sea stacked slate on the shore and pulled it down again. I was reminded of my last day and night in Australia. Only then Ragma had come along and provided a way out. In fair puzzles there should always be a way out. But I saw no doorways in the sand, and try as I might I could not make the puzzle fall fair.

"Well, Fred? Do you have something for us? Or should we go ahead? It is up to you now."

I looked at Mary, tied there in the chair. I tried not to look at her frightened face, look into her eyes, but I did. At my side, I heard Hal's heavy breathing stop short, as though he were tensing to spring. But Jamie Buckler noted this also, and the gun twitched slightly in his hand. Hal did not spring.

"Mister Zeemeister," I said, "If I had that stone, I would tie a bright ribbon around it and hand it to you. If I knew where it was, I would go get it for you or tell you where to find it. I do not want to see Mary dead, Hal dead, me dead. Ask me anything else and it's yours."

"Nothing else will do," he said, and he picked up the pliers.

We would be tortured and killed, if we just waited our turns. If we had had the answer and we gave it to them we would still be killed, though. Either way . . .

But we would not stand there and watch. We all knew that. We would try to rush them, and Mary and Hal and I would be the losers.

Wherever you are, whatever you are, I said in my shrillest thoughts, *if you can do something, do it now!*

Zeemeister had taken hold of Mary's wrist and forced her hand upward. As he reached for a finger with the pliers, the Ghost of Christmas Past or one of those guys drifted into the room behind him.

Stamping out of Jefferson Hall, cursing under my breath, I decided that a State Department official named Theodore Nadler was the next man I was going to punch in the eye. Making my way around the fountain and heading off toward the Student Union, however, I recalled that I had been remiss concerning my promise to call Hal in a day or so. I decided to phone him before I tried the Nadler number Wexroth had given me.

I picked up a coffee and doughnut before I made my way to the phone, realizing after thirteen years that all it took to make the Union's brew palatable was a reversal of every molecule in it, or in the drinker. I saw Ginny at a table off in the corner and my good intentions evaporated. I halted, started to turn in that direction. But then somebody moved and I saw that she was with a guy I didn't know. I decided to catch her another time, went on into the alcove. All the phones were in use, though, so I sipped my coffee and waited. Pace, pace. Sip, sip.

From behind my back I heard, "Hey, Cassidy! Come on, it's the guy I was telling you about!"

Turning, I saw Rick Liddy, an English major with an answer for everything except what to do with his degree come June. With him was a taller version of himself in a Yale sweatshirt.

"Fred, this is my brother Paul. He's come slumming," he said. "Hi, Paul."

I put my coffee on the ledge and started to extend the wrong hand. I caught myself, shook hands, felt foolish.

"He's the one," Rick said, "like the Wandering Jew or the Wild Huntsman. The man who will never graduate. Subject of countless ballads and limericks: Fred Cassidy—the Eternal Student."

"You left out the Flying Dutchman," I said, "and it's Doctor Cassidy, damn it!"

Rick began to laugh.

"Is it true about you being a night climber?" Paul said.

"Sometimes," I said, feeling a peculiar gulf opening between us. That damned sheepskin was already taking its toll. "Yeah, it's true."

"That's great," he said. "That's really great. I've always wanted to meet the real Fred Cassidy—the climber."

"I'm afraid you have," I said.

Then someone hung up and I grabbed for the phone.

"Excuse me."

"Yeah. See you later, Fred. Pardon me—Doc."

"Nice meeting you."

I felt strangely depressed as I wandered through the backward digits of Hal's number. As it was, the line proved busy. I tried the Nadler number then. An answering-service girl asked me for the number where I could be reached, for a message or for both. I gave her neither. I tried Hal's number again. This time I got through—within a fraction of a second, it seemed, from the time it commenced ringing.

"Yes? Hello?"

"You couldn't have run all that far," I said. "How come you're out of breath?"

"Fred! At last, damn it!"

"Sorry I didn't call sooner. There were a lot of things—"

"I've got to see you!"

"That's what I had in mind, too."

"Where are you?"

"At the Student Union."

"Stay there. No! Wait a minute."

I waited. Ten or fifteen seconds fell or were pushed.

"I'm trying to think of someplace you'll remember," he said. Then: "Listen. Don't say it if you do, but do you recall where we were about two months ago when you got in an argument with that med student named Ken? Thin guy, always very serious?"

"No," I said.

"I don't remember the argument, but I remember the ending: You said that Doctor Richard Jordan Gatling had done more for the development of modern surgery than Halsted. He asked you what techniques Doctor Gatling had developed and you told him that Gatling had invented the machine gun. He told you that wasn't funny and walked away. You told me he was an ass who believed he was going to get the Holy Grail when he finished rather than a license to help people. Do you remember where that was?"

"Now I do."

"Good. Go there, please. And wait."

"All right. I understand."

He hung up, then I did. Weird. And troubling. An obvious attempt to circumvent an eavesdropper's discovering where we were going to meet. Who? Why? And how many?

I departed the Union quickly, since I had mentioned it in our conversation. Headed north from the campus, three blocks. Then two blocks over and part way up a side street. It was a little bookstore I liked to visit about once a week, just to see what new titles had come in. Hal used to go along with me every now and then.

132

I browsed for perhaps half an hour, regarding the reversed titles in the backward shop. Occasionally, I paused to read a page or so of text for the practice of doing it that way—just in case things stayed topsy-turvy for any great length of time. The first sentence in one of The Dream Songs by John Berryman took on a peculiar, personal meaning:

> I stalk my mirror down this corridor
>   my pieces litter . . .

And I began thinking of the pieces of myself, scattered all over, from dronehood to raisinhood and thereafter. Was it worth it to stalk the mirror? I wondered. I had never really tried. But then—

I was considering buying the book when I felt a hand on my shoulder.

"Fred, come on."

"Hi, Hal. I was wondering—"

"Hurry," he said. "Please. I'm double-parked."

"Okay."

I restored the book to its rack and followed him out. I saw the car, went to it, got in. Hal climbed in his side and began driving. He did not say anything as he worked his way through the traffic, and since it was obvious that length of time. The first sentence in one of *Songs Dream* was ready to tell me about it. I lit a cigarette and stared out the window.

It took him several minutes to get us out of the sprawl and onto a more sedate stretch of road. It was only then that he spoke.

"In the note that you left you said that you had had a peculiar idea and were going to check it out. I take it that this involved the stone?"

"It involved the whole mess," I said, "so I guess the stone figures in, somehow. I am not at all sure how."

"Will you start at the beginning and tell me about it?"

"What about this urgent business of yours?"

"I want to hear everything that happened to you first. All right?"

"All right. Where are we going, anyway?"

"Just driving for now. Please, tell me everything, from the time you left my place through today."

So I did. I talked and I talked and the buildings all ran away after a time and the grasses rushed up to the roadside, grew taller, were joined by shrubbery, tentative trees, an occasional cow, boulders and random jack rabbits. Hal listened, nodded, asked a question every now and then, kept driving.

"Then, say, right now, it looks to you as if I'm driving from the wrong side of the car?" he asked.

"Yes."

"Fascinating."

I saw then that we were nearing the ocean, moving through an area dotted by summer cottages, mostly deserted this time of year. I had gotten so involved in my story that I had not realized we had been driving for close to an hour.

"And you've got a bona fide doctorate now?"

"That's what I said."

"Very strange."

"Hal, you're stalling. What's the matter? What is it that you don't want to tell me?"

"Look in the back seat," he said.

"Okay. It's full of junk, as usual. You should really clean it out some——"

"The jacket in the corner. It's wrapped in my jacket."

I brought the jacket up front and unrolled it.

"The stone! Then you had it all along!"

"No, I didn't," he said.

"Then where did you find it? Where was it?"

Hal turned up a side road. A pair of gulls dipped past.

"Study it," he said. "Look at it carefully. That's it, isn't it?"

"Sure looks like it. But I never really scrutinized it before."

"It has to be it," he said. "Believe that I just found it in the bottom of a trunk I hadn't unpacked till now. Stick to that."

"What do you mean, 'Stick to that'?"

"I got into Byler's lab last night and took it from the shelf. There were several. It's just as good as the one he gave us. You can't tell the difference, can you?"

"No, but I'm no expert. What's going on?"

"Mary has been kidnapped," he said.

I looked over at him. His face was expressionless, which was the way I knew it would be if something like that were true.

"When? How?"

"We'd had a misunderstanding and she had gone home to her mother's, that night you stopped over . . ."

"Yes, I remember."

"Well, I was going to call the next day and try to smooth things over. But the more I considered it the more I kept thinking how much nicer it would be if she called me first. I'd have some sort of little moral victory that way, I decided. So I waited. I came close to phoning a number of times, but I'd always put it off just a little longer—hoping she would call. She didn't, though, and I had let it get fairly late. Too late, really. So I decided to give it another night. I did, and then I called her mother's place in the morning. Not only was she not there, but she hadn't been there at all. Her mother hadn't even heard from her. I figured, okay, she has good sense. She had had second thoughts, didn't want to turn the thing into a family issue. She had changed her mind and gone to stay with one of her girl friends. I started calling them. Nothing.

"Then, between calls," he went on, "someone called me. It was a man, and he asked if I knew where my wife was. My first thought was that there had been an accident of some sort. But he said that she was all right, that he would even let me talk to her in a minute. They were holding her. They had held her for a day to make me sweat. Now they were going to tell me what they wanted in return for her release, unharmed."

"The stone, of course."

"Of course. And also, of course, he did not believe me when I said I did not have it. He told me they would give me a day in which to get hold of it, and when they got in touch with me again they would tell me what to do with it. Then he let me talk to Mary. She said she was all right, but she sounded scared. I told him not to hurt her, and I promised to look for it. Then I started searching. I looked through everything that I have. No stone. Then I tried your place. I still have my key."

"Anybody there toasting the Queen?"

"No signs of your visitors at all. Then I proceeded to look for the stone in every possible place. Finally, I gave up. It's just gone, that's all."

He grew silent. We twisted along the narrow road, occasional glimpses of the sea appearing through gaps in the foliage off to my left/his right.

"So?" I said. "What then?"

"He called again the next day, asked if I had it. I told him I did not—and he said they were going to kill Mary. I pleaded with him, said I'd do anything—"

"Wait. You did not call the police?"

He shook his head.

"He told me not to—the first time that we talked. Any sort of police involvement, he said, and I would never see her again. I thought about calling the cops, but I was scared. If I called the police and he found out . . . I just couldn't take the chance. What would you have done?"

"I don't know," I said. "But go ahead. What happened next?"

"He asked me if I knew where you were, said you could probably help find it—"

"Ha! Sorry. Go on."

"Again, I had to tell him I did not know but that I was expecting to hear from you soon. He said they would give me another day to find the stone or to find you. Then he hung up. Later, I thought about the stones in Paul's lab, got to wondering whether any of them were still there. If they were, why not try to pass one off as the real thing? They were obviously good fakes. The man who made them had even been fooled by one himself for a time. I was able to force the lock and get into his lab later in the day. I was desperate enough to try anything. There were four of them on the shelf, and I took the one you are holding now. I took it home with me and I waited. He phoned me again this morning—right before you called—and I told him I had come across it in the bottom of an old trunk. He sounded happy then. He even let me talk to Mary again and she said she was still okay. He told me where to take the stone, said they would meet me and make the exchange—her for it."

"And that is where we are headed now?"

"Yes. I would not have involved you needlessly, but they seemed so convinced that you were something of an authority on the thing that when you called it occurred to me that if you were there to corroborate my story there would be no question as to the stone's authenticity. I didn't like involving you this way, but it is a matter of life and death."

"Yeah. They may kill us all."

"Why should they? They will have what they want. It would be pointless to harm us."

"Witnesses," I said.

"To what? It would be our word against theirs that the incident even occurred. There is no record of it, no evidence of a kidnapping or anything else. Why jeopardize the status quo by killing people and starting a homicide investigation?"

"The whole thing stinks, that's why. We do not have sufficient facts to decide what may or may not be motivating them."

"What else was I to do? Call the police and take a chance they might not be bluffing?"

"I already said that I don't know. But at the risk of sounding ignoble, you might have left me out of this."

"Sorry," he said. "It was a quick judgment and maybe a wrong one. But I was not rushing you there blind. I knew I owed you an explanation, and that is what I have been giving you. We are not there yet. There is still time to drop you off if you do not want to be party to it. I intended to offer you the choice when I finished explaining things. Now that I have, you can make up your own mind about it. I had to hurry, though."

He glanced at his watch.

"When are we supposed to meet them?" I asked.

"About half an hour."

"Where?"

"Around eight miles, I think. I'm going by landmarks they gave me. Then we park it and wait."

"I see. I don't suppose you recognized the voice, or anything like that?"

"No."

I looked down at the pseudostone, semiopaque or semitransparent, depending on one's philosophy and vision, very smooth, shot with milky streaks and red ones. It somewhat resembled a fossil sponge or a seven-limbed branch of coral, polished smooth as glass and tending to glitter about its tips and junctures. Tiny black and yellow flecks were randomly distributed throughout. It was about seven inches long and three across. It felt heavier than it looked.

"Nice piece of work, this," I said. "I can't tell it from the other. Yes, I'll go with you."

"Thanks."

We drove on, maybe eight miles. I watched the scenery and wondered what was going to happen. Hal turned down an ill-tended car trail—I could not really call it a road—very near to the beach. He parked the car at the edge of a marshy area, in a place where the trees screened us on all sides. Then we got out, lit cigarettes and waited. I could hear the sea from where we stood, smell it, taste it. The soil was gritty, the air was clammy. I rested my foot on a log and stared into the stagnant wash, spindled and mutilated by reeds and reflection.

Several cigarettes later, Hal looked at his watch again.

"They're late," he said.

I shrugged.

"Probably watching right now to make sure we're alone," I said. "I would—for a long while. I would probably have a spotter back on the road, too."

"Sounds likely," he agreed. "I'm getting tired of standing. I'm going to sit in the car again."

I turned also, and we saw Jamie Buckler standing near the rear of the car, regarding us. He appeared to be unarmed, but then there was no necessity for him to flash a weapon. He knew we would do whatever he said without additional coercion.

"Are you the one who called?" Hal asked, advancing.

"Yes. Have you got it?"

"Is she all right?"

"She's fine. Have you got it?"

Hal halted and unwrapped the stone. He displayed it on his jacket.

"Here. See?"

"Yeah. Okay. Come on. Bring it along."

"Where?"

"Not far. Do an about-face and head that way," he said, gesturing. "There's a little trail."

We moved off along the route he had indicated, Jamie bringing up the rear. Winding through scrub, it took us farther down toward the beach. Finally, I got a closeup view of the sea, gray today and white-capped. Then the trail took us away again, and before very long I thought I had spotted our destination—low, peaked, set back on a modest hillside, missing a shutter and a half—a beach cottage that had seen better seas before I was born.

"The cottage?" Hal said.

"The cottage" from behind us.

We went on up to it. Jamie circled about us, rapped in a doubtless prearranged fashion and said, "It's okay. It's me. He's got it. He brought Cassidy along, too."

An "Okay" emerged from inside, and he opened the door and turned to us. He gestured with his head and we moved past him and on in.

I was not exactly taken by surprise to see Morton Zeemeister seated at the scarred kitchen table, a gun beside his coffee cup. Across the room beyond the kitchenette area, Mary was seated in what looked to be the most comfortable chair in the place. She was tied loosely, but one hand was free and there was a cup of coffee on the table beside her also. There were two windows in the dining area and two in the living room. In the rear wall there were two doors—a bedroom and a john or closet, I guessed. The overhead area had not been floored or ceiled, and there were only bare beams and lots of space, where someone had stashed fishing gear, nets, oars and assorted junk. There was an old sofa, a couple more rickety chairs and low tables and a pair of lamps in the living room. Also a dead fireplace and a faded rug. The kitchenette held a small stove, refrigerator, cupboards and a black cat who sat licking her paws at the far end of the table from Zeemeister.

He smiled as we entered, raising the gun only when Hal began a dash toward Mary.

"Come back here," he said. "She is all right."

"Are you?" Hal asked her.

"Yes," she said. "They didn't hurt me."

Mary is a small, somewhat flighty girl, blond and a trifle too sharp-featured for my tastes. I had feared she would be somewhat hysterical by then. But, outside of the expected signs of stress and fatigue, she seemed possessed of a stability that exceeded my expectations. Hal might have done better than I had thought. I was glad.

Hal returned from her side, moved toward the table. I glanced back when I heard the door shut, its latch clicking into place. Jamie leaned there, his back against the frame, watching us. He had opened his jacket, and I saw that there was a gun tucked in behind his belt.

"Let's have it," Zeemeister said.

Hal unwrapped it again and passed it to him.

Zeemeister pushed aside his gun and coffee cup. He placed the stone before him and stared at it. He turned it several times. The cat rose, stretched, jumped down from the table.

He leaned back in his chair then, still looking at the stone.

"You boys must have gone to a lot of trouble—" he began.

"As a matter of fact," Hal stated, "we—"

Zeemeister slammed the table with the palm of his hand. The crockery danced.

"It's a fake!" he said.

"It's the same one we've always had," I offered, but Hal had turned bright red. He is a lousy poker player, too.

"I don't see how you can say that!" Hal shouted. "I've brought you the damned thing! It's real! Let her go now!"

Jamie moved away from the door, coming up beside Hal. At that moment, Zeemeister turned his head and raised his eyes. He shook his head slightly, just once, and Jamie halted.

"I am not a fool," he said, "to be taken in by a copy. I know what it is that I want and I am capable of recognizing it. This—" he made a flipping motion with his right hand—"is not it. You know that as well as I do. It was a good try, because it is a good copy. But you have played your last trick. Where is the real one?"

"If that is not it," Hal said, "then I do not know."

"What about you, Fred?"

"That is the one we have had all along," I said. "If it is a fake, then we never had the real one."

"All right."

He heaved himself to his feet.

"Get on over into the living room," he said, picking up his gun.

At this, Jamie drew his own and we moved to obey.

"I do not know how much you think you can get for it," Zeemeister said, "or how much you may have been offered. Or, for that matter, whether you have already sold it. Whatever the case, you are going to tell me where the stone is now and who else is involved. Above all, I want you to bear in mind that it is worth nothing to you if you are dead. Right now, it looks like that is what is going to happen."

"You are making a mistake," Hal said.

"No. You have made it, and now the innocent must suffer."

"What do you mean by that?" Hal asked.

"It should be obvious," he replied. Then: "Stand there," he directed, "and don't move. Jamie, shoot them if they do."

We halted where he had indicated, across the room from Mary. He continued, moving to stand at her right side. Jamie crossed over to her left and waited there, covering us.

"How about you, Fred?" Zeemeister asked. "Do you recall anything now that you didn't in Australia? Perhaps remember

142

something you haven't even bothered mentioning to poor Hal here—something that could save his wife from . . . Well . . ."

He removed a pair of pliers from his pocket and placed them on the table beside her coffee cup. Hal turned and looked at me. They all waited for me to say something, do something. I glanced out the side window and wondered about doorways in the sand.

The apparition entered silently from the room behind them. It must have been Hal's face that gave them the first sign, because I know I kept mine under control. It did not really matter, though, because it spoke even as Zeemeister's head was turning.

"No!" it said, and "Freeze! Drop it, Jamie! One bloody move for your gun, Morton, and you'll look like a statue by that Henry Moore chap! Just stay still!"

It was Paul Byler in a dark coat, his face thinner and sporting a few new creases. His hand was steady, though, and it was a .45 that he was pointing. Zeemeister assumed an eloquent immobility. Jamie looked undecided, glanced at Zeemeister for some sign.

I almost sighed, feeling something tending in the direction of relief. In fair puzzles there should always be a way out. This looked like it for this game, if only—

Catastrophe!

A mass of lines, nets, buoys and disassembled fishing poles made a scratching, sliding noise overhead, then descended on Paul. His head jerked upward, his arm swayed—and in that moment Jamie decided against discarding his gun. He swung it toward Paul.

Reflexes I usually forget about when I am on the ground made a decision for which I take neither credit nor blame. Had the matter gotten beyond my spinal nerves, though, I do not believe I would have jumped a man with a gun.

But then everything was going to turn out all right, wasn't it? It always does in the various mass-entertainment media.

I sprang toward Jamie, my arms outstretched.

His hand slowed in an instant's indecision, then swung the gun back toward me and fired it, point-blank.

My chest exploded and the world went away.

So much for mass entertainment.

9

IT IS GOOD TO PAUSE PERIODICALLY and reflect on the benefits to be derived from the modern system of higher education.

I guess it can all be laid at the feet of my patron saint, President Eliot of Harvard. It was he who, back in the 1870s, felt that it would be nice to loosen the academic strait jacket a bit. He did this, and he also forgot to lock the door when he left the room. For nearly thirteen years I had granted him my gratitude once every month in that emotion-charged moment when I opened the envelope containing my allowance check. He it was who introduced the elective system, a modest tonic at the time, to a rigid course of forbidding curricula. And, as is sometimes the case with tonics, the results were contagious. And mutable. Their current incarnation, for example, permitted me to rest full-burnished, not grow dull in use, while following the winking star of knowledge. In other words, if it were not for him I might never have had time and opportunity to explore such things as the delightful and instructive habits of *Ophrys speculum* and *Cryptostylis leptochila*, whom I encountered in a botany seminar I would otherwise have been denied. Look at it that way. I owed the man my life-style and many of the agreeable things that filled it. And

I am not ungrateful. As with any form of indebtedness impossible to repay, I acknowledge it freely.

And who is Ophrys? What is she? That all our swains commend her? And Cryptostylis? I am glad that you asked. In Algeria there lives a wasplike insect known as *Scolia ciliata*. He sleeps for a time in his burrow in a sandbank, awakens and emerges around March. The female of the species, following a fashion not peculiar to the hymenoptera, remains abed for another month. Her mate understandably grows restless, begins to cast his myopic gaze about the countryside. And lo! What should be blooming at that time in that very vicinity but the dainty orchid *Ophrys speculum*, with flowers that amazingly resemble the body of the female of the insect's species. The rest is quite predictable. And this is the fashion in which the orchid achieves its pollination, as he goes from flower to flower, paying his respects. Pseudocopulation is what Oakes Ames called it, the symbiotic association of two different reproductive systems. And the orchid *Cryptostylis leptochila* seduces the male ichneumonid wasp, *Lissopimpla semipunctata*, in the same fashion, for the same purpose, with the added finesse of producing an odor like that of the female wasp. Insidious. Delightful. Morals galore, in a strict philosophical sense. This is what education is all about. Were it not for my dear, stiff Uncle Albert and President Eliot, I might have been denied such experiences and the light they constantly shed on my own condition.

For example, as I lay there, still uncertain as to where *there* was, a couple of the lessons of the orchid drifted through my mind, along with unclassified sounds and unsorted shapes and colors. I quickly achieved such conclusions as, things are not always what they seem, and sometimes it doesn't matter; and one can get screwed in the damnedest ways, often involving the spinal nerves.

I was testing my environment in a tentative fashion by then.

"Ooow! Ooww!" and "Owww!" I said—for how long I am uncertain—when the environment finally responded by sticking a thermometer in my mouth and taking my pulse.

"You awake, Mister Cassidy?" a feminine-to-neuter voice inquired.

"Glab," I replied, bringing the nurse's face into focus and letting it go back out of focus again after I had gotten a good look.

"You are a very lucky man, Mister Cassidy," she said, withdrawing the thermometer. "I am going to get hold of the doctor now. He is quite anxious to talk with you. Lie still. Don't exert yourself."

In that I felt no particular urge to roll over and do pushups, it was not difficult to comply with this last. I did do the focus-trick again, though, and this time everything stayed put. Everything consisted of what appeared to be a private hospital room, with me on the bed by the wall by the window. I lay flat on my back and quickly discovered the extent to which my chest was swathed with gauze and tape. I winced at the thought of the dressings' eventual removal. The unmaimed do not have a monopoly on anticipation.

Moments later, it seemed, a husky young man in the usual white, stethoscope spilling out of his pocket, pushed a smile into the room and brought it near. He transferred a clipboard from one hand to the other and reached toward my own. I thought he was going to take my pulse, but instead he clasped my hand and shook it.

"Mister Cassidy, I'm Doctor Drade," he said. "We met earlier, but you don't remember it. I operated on you. Glad to see that your handshake is that strong. You are a very lucky man."

I coughed and it hurt.

"That's good to know," I said.

He raised the clipboard.

"Since your hand is in such good shape," he said, "may I have your signature on some release forms I have here?"

"Just a minute," I said. "I don't even know what's been done to me. I am not about to okay it at this point."

"Oh, it is not that sort of release," he said. "They'll get that when you are checking out. This just gives me permission to use your medical record and some photos I was fortunate enough to obtain during surgery as part of an article I want to write."

"What sort of article?" I asked.

"One involving the reason I said you are a very lucky man. You were shot in the chest, you know."

"I had sort of figured that out myself."

"Anyone else would probably be dead as a result. But not good old Fred Cassidy. Do you know why not?"

"Tell me."

"Your heart is in the wrong place."

"Oh."

"Have you actually gotten this far along in life without becoming aware of the peculiar anatomy of your circulatory system?"

"Not exactly," I said. "But then, I've never been shot in the chest before either."

"Well, your heart is a mirror image of an average, garden-variety heart. The vena cavae feed from the left and the pulmonary artery receives the blood from your left ventricle. Your pulmonary veins take the fresh blood to the right auricle, and the right ventricle pumps it through an aortic arch that swings over to the right. The right chambers of your heart consequently have the thick-walled development other people have on the left side. Now, anyone else shot in the same place you were would probably have been hit in the left ventricle, or possibly the aorta. In your case, though, the bullet went harmlessly past the inferior vena cava."

I coughed again.

"Well, relatively harmlessly," he amended. "There is still a hole, of course. I've patched it neatly, though. You should be back on your feet in no time."

"Great."

"Now, about the releases . . ."

"Yeah. Okay. Anything for science and progress and all that."

While I was signing the papers and wondering about the angle of the bullet, I asked him, "What were the circumstances involved in my being brought here?"

"You were brought to the emergency room by the police," he said. "They did not inform us as to the nature of the, uh, situation that led to the shootings."

"Shootings? How many of us were there?"

"Well, seven altogether. I am not really supposed to discuss other cases, you know."

I paused in mid-signature.

"Hal Sidmore is my best friend," I said, raising the pen and glancing significantly at the forms, "and his wife's name is Mary."

"They were not seriously injured," he said quickly. "Mister Sidmore has a broken arm and his wife has a few scratches. That is the extent of it. In fact, he has been waiting to see you."

"I want to see him," I said. "I feel up to it."

"I'll send him in shortly."

"Very good."

I finished signing and returned his pen and papers.

"Could I be raised a bit?" I asked.

"I don't see why not."

He adjusted the bed.

"And if I could trouble you for a glass of water . . ."

He poured me one, waited while I drank most of it.

"Okay," he said, "I'll be in to see you later. Would you mind if I brought some interns along to listen to your heart?"

"Not if you promise to send me a copy of your article."

"All right," he said, "I will. Don't do anything strenuous."

"I'll keep that in mind."

He folded his smile and went away and I lay there grimacing at the ᴎo sᴍoкиɴɢ sign.

It wasn't too much later, I guess, that Hal wandered in. Another layer of dopiness and confusion had peeled away by then. He was dressed in his street clothes, and his right arm—wait a minute, pardon me—left arm was in a sling. He also had a small bruise on his forehead.

I grinned, to show him that life was beautiful, and since I already knew the answer was all right, I asked, "How's Mary?"

"Great," he said. "Real good. Shook up and scratched, but nothing serious. How about yourself?"

"Feels like a jackass kicked me in the chest," I said. "But the doctor tells me it could have been worse."

"Yes, he said you were very lucky. He's in love with your heart, by the way. If it were mine, I'd be a little uncomfortable—all helpless like that, with him writing the prescriptions . . ."

"Thanks. I'm sure glad you came by to cheer me up. Are you going to tell me what happened, or do I have to buy a paper?"

"I didn't realize you were in a hurry," he said. "I'll be brief, then. We were all shot."

"I see. Now be less brief."

"All right. You jumped at the man with the gun—"

"Jamie. Yes. Go on."

"He shot you. You fell. Put a check mark next to your name. Then he shot Paul."

"Check."

"But, while Jamie was turned toward you, Paul had gotten partly clear of the junk that had fallen on him. He fired at Jamie at about the same time Jamie fired at him. He hit Jamie."

"So they shot each other. Check."

"I went for the other guy just a little after you lunged at Jamie."

"Zeemeister. Yes."

"He had his gun by then and got off several shots. The first one missed me. Then we wrestled around. He's damn strong, by the way."

"I know that. Who do I check next?"

"I am not certain. Mary had her scalp grazed by a shot or a ricochet, and his second or third shot—I'm not sure which— got me in the arm."

"Two checks, either way. Who shot Zeemeister?"

"A cop. They came busting in about then."

"Why were they there? How did they know what was going on?"

"I overheard them talking afterwards. They had been following Paul—"

"—who had been following us, perhaps?"

"It seems so."

"But I thought he was dead. It made the news."

"That makes two of us. I still don't know the story. His room is guarded and no one is talking."

"He is *still* alive then?"

"Last I heard. But that was all I could learn about him. It seems we all made it."

"Too bad—twice anyway. Wait a minute. Doctor Drade said there were seven shootings."

"Yes. It was sort of embarrassing to them: One of the police shot himself in the foot."

"Oh. That's all the checks, then. What else?"

"What else what?"

"Did you learn anything from all this? Like, about the stone?"

"Nope. Nothing. You know everything I do."

"Unfortunate."

I began to yawn uncontrollably. About then the nurse looked in.

"I'm going to have to ask you to leave," she said. "We can't tire him."

"Yes, all right," he told her. "I'm going home now, Fred. I'll come back as soon as they say I can see you again. Can I bring you anything?"

"Is there any oxygen equipment in here?"

"No. It's out in the hall."

"Cigarettes, then. And tell them to take that damned sign down. Never mind. I will. Excuse me. I can't stop. Give Mary my sympathy and such. Hope she doesn't have a headache. Did I ever tell you about the flowers that lay wasps?"

"No."

"I'm afraid you will have to go now," the nurse said.

"All right."

"Tell that lady she's no orchid," I said, "even if she does make me feel waspish," and I slipped back down to the still soft center of things where life was simpler by far, and the bed got lowered there.

Drowse. Drowse, drowse.

Glimmer?

Glimmer. Also glitter and shine.

I heard the noises of arrival in my room and opened my eyelids just enough to show me it was still daytime.

Still?

I totted up my times. A day and a night and a piece of another day had passed. I had eaten several meals, talked with Doctor Drade and been auscultated by the interns. Hal had come back, happier, left me cigarettes which Drade had told me I could smoke against his wishes, which I did. Then I had slept some more. Oh yes, there I was . . .

Two figures passed into my slitted field of vision, moving slowly. The throat-clearing sounds which then occurred were Drade's.

Finally: "Mister Cassidy, are you awake?" he seemed to wonder aloud.

I yawned and stretched and pretended to come around while I assessed the situation. Beside Drade stood a tall, somber-looking individual. The dark suit and smoked glasses did that for him. I suppressed a wisecrack about morticians when I saw that the man's right hand was wrapped about a guide harness attached to a scruffy-looking dog that tried to sit at attention beside him. In his left hand the man held the handle of a heavy-looking case.

"Yes," I said, reaching for the controls and raising myself to sit facing them. "What's up?"

"How do you feel?"

"All right, I guess. Yes. Rested."

"Good. The police have sent this gentleman along to talk with you about whatever it is they are interested in. He has requested privacy, so we will hang a sign on the door. His name is Nadler, Theodore Nadler. I'll leave you alone now."

He guided Nadler to a visitor's chair, saw him seated and left, closing the door behind him.

I took a drink of water. I looked at Nadler.

"What do you want?" I said.

"You know what we want."

"Try running an ad," I suggested.

He removed his glasses and smiled at me.

"Try reading a few. Like 'Help Wanted.' "

"You ought to be in the diplomatic corps," I said, and his smile went tight and his face reddened.

I smiled then as he sighed.

"We know that you do not have it, Cassidy," he finally said, "and I am not asking you for it."

"Then why push me around the way you have? Just because I'm pushable? You've really shot me down, you know, forcing that degree on me. If I did have anything that you wanted there would be a big price tag on it now."

"How big?" he said, just a little too quickly.

"For what?"

"Your services."

"In what capacity?"

"We were thinking of offering you a job you might find interesting. How would you like to become an alien culture specialist for the U.S. legation to the United Nations? The job description calls for a Ph.D. in anthropology."

"When was the job description written?" I asked.

He smiled again.

"Fairly recently."

"I see. And what would the duties be?"

"They would commence with a special assignment, of an investigatory nature."

"Investigating what?"

"The disappearance of the star-stone."

"Uh-huh. Well, I have to admit that the matter appeals to my curiosity," I said, "but not so much that I would be willing to work for you."

"You would not actually be working for me."

I got hold of my cigarettes and lit one before I asked, "For whom, then?"

"Give me one of those," said a familiar voice, and the scruffy-looking dog rose and crossed over to my bedside.

"The Lon Chaney of the interstellar set," I observed. "You make a lousy dog, Ragma."

He unsnapped several sections of his disguise and accepted a light. I could not make out what he looked like inside.

"So you went and got yourself shot again," he said. "It is not as if you had not been warned."

"That is correct," I said. "I did it with my eyes open."

"And reversed," he said, pushing aside my blanket and staring downward. "The scars are on the wrong leg for the wounds you sustained in Australia."

He let the blanket fall and went to hunker beside my table.

"Not that I needed to look," he added. "I overheard things about your wonderful reversed heart on the way in. And I sort of felt all along that you had to be the idiot who was fooling around with the inversion unit. Mind telling me why?"

"Yes," I said, "I would mind."

He shrugged.

"All right. It is still a bit early for malnutrition. I'll wait."

I looked back at Nadler.

"You still haven't answered my question," I said. "For whom would I be working?"

This time he grinned.

"Him," he said.

"Are you kidding? When did the State Department start hiring wombat impersonators and guide dogs? Nonresident alien ones, at that?"

"Ragma is not a State Department employee. He is lending his services to the United Nations. On coming to work for us you would immediately go on loan to the special UN task force he heads."

"Sort of like a library book," I said, looking back toward Ragma. "Do you want to tell me about it?"

"That is why I am here," he said. "As you are obviously aware, the artifact generally known as the starstone is missing. You were apparently in possession of it for a time, and as a consequence you are the focus of interest for a number of parties concerned with its recovery—for a variety of reasons."

"Paul Byler had it?"

"Yes. He was commissioned to construct a display model."

"Then he was pretty careless with it."

"Yes and no. A most peculiar man, Professor Byler, and the subject of a coincidence that complicated matters in a fashion that could not have been foreseen. You see, he was approached to undertake the job because he was considered one of the best qualified persons about for that sort of work. He had done all manner of clever things involving synthetics and crystals and such in the past. And he produced a beautiful specimen, one that a reviewing board was actually incapable of distinguishing from the supposed original. A tribute to the man's skill? So it seemed, at first. I do not know how the deception could have been uncovered by your people in the ordinary course of events."

"He kept the original and gave them back a copy, along with a copy of the copy?"

"Nothing quite that simple," Ragma said. "As it turned out, the object they gave him to duplicate was not the star-stone. A substitution had actually taken place much earlier—within minutes, as we understand it now, of the formal receipt of the stone by the Secretary General of the United Nations. Perhaps you saw that event televised?"

"I guess everyone did. What happened?"

"One of the guards exchanged it for a false stone while conveying it to the vault. The exchange went undetected, he made off with the genuine item and Professor Byler received the counterfeit for duplication."

"Then how could Paul have any part in . . .?"

"The coincidence," he said, "the one coincidence allowable in every story. I am surprised that you did not ask me where the guard obtained the ringer."

I sagged slightly. I wondered whether it would hurt my chest much if I laughed.

"Not. . . Paul?" I said. "Tell me he didn't make the first counterfeit."

"But he did," said Ragma. "Just from a few advance photos and a written description. Now *there* is a tribute to his skill. When it came to technique, he really was the best choice."

I mashed out my cigarette.

"So he got his own counterfeit back to counterfeit?"

"Precisely. Which placed him in a very awkward position. There he was with the real thing, working on an improved counterfeit, now that he had something better than photos and descriptions to go on, and the UN approached him to duplicate his original work."

"Wait! He had the real one? I thought the guard had taken the real one."

"I was just getting to that. The guard removed it and transported it to Professor Byler. Byler was afraid that the first counterfeit would not stand close scrutiny, especially from some visiting alien who might have seen it elsewhere and known something concerning its physical makeup—something which perhaps only an alien could detect. At any rate, his intention was to produce a superior replica the second time around and then have the same guard try to exchange it for his earlier model. The second version, he believed, could stand scrutiny for a much longer while. So he was faced with a dilemma at that point: Give them back the first one and a copy, or give them two of the second-generation stones of which he was quite proud. He resolved it by returning the first one and a copy, as he feared the authorities might by then have done a detailed study of its properties and have them on record as its authentic specifications."

I shook my head.

"But why? Why go through the whole rigamarole in the first place?"

Ragma put out his cigarette and sighed.

"The man possesses a powerful emotional commitment to the British monarchy—"

"The crown jewels!" I said.

"Exactly. The star-stone came and they went. He was obsessed by their departure, by what he considered the unfairness of the deal, the insult to the sovereign."

"But they are, in effect, still theirs and still available. The British approved their indefinite loan under those terms."

"We both seem to see it that way," Ragma said. "He does not. Neither do some of those—such as the guard—who cooperated with him in the venture."

"What, specifically, did they plan on doing?"

"Their intention was to wait for a time, until your relations with the other races had broadened and the benefits of this association had become firmly fixed in the public mind. At that point they would announce that the star-stone was a fake—a fact readily verifiable by extraterrestrial authorities—and then proclaim that they were holding the real one to ransom. The price, of course, was to be the return of the crown jewels."

"So a screwball group was behind it. That even explains a certain toast I overheard in my apartment. They were doubtless waiting to question me, to learn where to go to steal it back again."

"Yes. They have been looking for you. But then we have them under surveillance. They are more a nuisance than a threat, actually, and they might possibly even help us to locate the stone if we leave them unmolested. This seems enough to offset the inconveniences involved."

"What would have happened if everything had gone as they planned it?"

"If the scheme succeeded, then the Earth would be expelled from the trading cycle and probably be blacklisted for normal trade, tourism and cultural and scientific exchanges. It would also seriously impair your chances of eventually being invited to join the formal confederation we possess, an organization roughly equivalent to your own United Nations."

"And an intelligent man like Paul can't understand this? It makes me wonder whether we are ready for something of that scope."

"Oh, he does now. He is the one who gave us all the details as to what had occurred. And do not be too hard on him. Matters of sentiment are seldom mediated by the intellect."

"What happened in his case, anyway? I had heard that he had been killed."

"He had been attacked and severely abused, but police happened on the scene just as his assailants were departing. They possessed medical equipment to supply immediate emergency aid, and they rushed him to a facility where he underwent a number of organ implants, all of which proved successful. Thereafter, he contacted the authorities and told the entire story. His change of heart was prompted by the fact that his attackers had formerly been associates of his."

"Zeemeister and Buckler," I said, "did not strike me as the sort whose intellects are mediated by sentiment."

"True. They are, basically, hoodlums. Until recently their major activities had involved organ procurement and smuggling. Before that they had done many other illicit things, but organs seem to have been going well recently. They were involved in the theft of the star-stone for monetary rather than idealistic reasons. None of the other members of the conspiracy were criminals in the professional sense of the term. This was why they hired Zeemeister—to plan the theft for them. His ultimate design, however, involved a brace of roods—"

"Doublecross," I said, lighting another cigarette for him.

"Just so. He intended to appropriate the stone for himself somewhere along the line and restore it to the authorities in return for money and immunity from prosecution."

"If that were to happen, how would it affect our chances with respect to eventual membership in the confederation?"

"It would not be as harmful as the use of it for the recovery of the crown jewels," he said. "So long as you have it ready to pass along at the appropriate time, any intervening problems concerning its maintenance are your own concern."

"Then what is your real part in this affair?"

"I do not like to look at things so terribly strictly," he said. "You are new to the game, and I want to see that you get every break possible. I would like to see the stone recovered and the entire incident forgotten."

"Decent of you," I said, "so I will try to be reasonable. I assume that Paul retained the original stone and that he has told you he believes it passed into our custody during a certain card party in his lab."

"That is correct."

"So Hal and I possibly, even probably, had it in our apartment for a time. And then it vanished."

"So it would seem."

"What then, specifically, would you want me to do about it if I took this job?"

"Of first importance," he said, "since you do not wish to go offworld to be examined by a telepathic analyst and since Sibla's qualifications do not meet with your approval, I would like you to consent to the procedure in the case of my bringing a qualified person here to Earth."

"So you still think a clue might be locked away somewhere in my mind?"

"We have to admit the possibility, do we not?"

"Yes. I guess we do. What about Hal? Maybe he has something at some buried level, too."

"There is that possibility also, though I am inclined to believe him when he insists as he does that he left the stone behind. However, he has just recently given his consent to Mister Nadler to go along with any sort of mind-probing technique that may be of help."

"Then I do, too. Bring on your analyst. Just so he knows his business and is in no position to lock me away on another world."

"All right. That is settled, then. Does it mean you are accepting the job?"

"Why not? I might as well get paid for it—especially if the checks will be coming from the people who messed up my normal means of livelihood."

"Then we will leave it at that for now. It will require several days for the transportation of the analyst I have located. For now, Mister Nadler has some forms and such for your signature. While you are dealing with these, I will be setting up a unit we have brought along."

"What sort of equipment is it?"

"Your leg healed up nicely, did it not?"

"Yes."

"I am prepared to do the same for your chest wound. You should be able to leave here this evening."

"That would be most welcome. Then what?"

"Then you have only to remain out of trouble for a few days. This can be achieved either by locking you up or by keeping you under reasonable surveillance, with the understanding that you will seek to avoid troublesome situations. I assume you would prefer the latter."

"You assume correctly."

"Then fill out the papers. I am going to warm up the unit and put you to sleep shortly."

Which is what happened.

Later, as they were preparing to leave—all the medical gear and standard forms stashed, Nadler in his shades, Ragma back in harness—Ragma turned and said to me, almost too casually, "By the way, now that we have achieved something of an understanding, would you care to tell me why you got yourself reversed?"

And I was about to. There seemed no reason for withholding any of that slice of affairs, now that we were together in this thing, so to speak. I decided that I might as well tell him.

I opened my mouth, but the words did not assemble themselves and emerge properly. I felt a tiny constriction in my throat, a certain thickness at the base of my tongue and a spontaneous flexion of various facial muscles as I smiled faintly, nodded slightly and then said, "I'd rather go into that a bit later, all right? Say tomorrow or the next day?"

"All right," he said. "No great urgency. When the time comes, we can reverse the reversal. Rest now, eat everything they give you and see how you feel. Mister Nadler or I will be in touch later in the week. Good afternoon."

"So long."

"We'll be seeing you," Nadler said.

They left the door slightly ajar behind them. I did not doubt for a moment that I still lacked the entire story. But then, so did they. I had just been willing to level with them and my body had handed me a brace of roods. I found this especially frightening because in some ways it reminded me of my experience on the bus ride home. I could still see the marks of concern on the old man's brow as he asked me if I were feeling all right. Was it a similar thing that had taken me just now, a bizarre repercussion on my nervous system? An effect of the reversal? The timing was so smooth, though . . . I did not like it at all. Nothing I had ever come across in my checkered study of man and his manifold ways seemed of assistance at that moment.

President Eliot, we got problems.

10

As THE CABLELIKE VINES or tentacles seized me, thigh and shoulder, hoisting me into the air to a position where, wrenching my neck, I was afforded a view of the thing's massive trunk, down to where it emerged from the tub of slime in the center of the room, I reflected, as the enormous Venus's-flytrap-type blades snapped open, revealing a reddish interior, that while it may be true that most accidents are caused by carelessness, I could in no way be held responsible this time. Since my departure from the hospital I had been a model State Department employee, totally circumspect in thought and deed.

As it paused for an instant, perhaps debating the best disposition of the alkaloids my excess nitrogen would provide, the past couple of days flashed before me. No more than that, as I was still fresh on the earlier portions of my life from the last time I had been about to die.

I don't know whether it was that certain smile or morbid curiosity that manipulated me next. Doctor Drade had wanted to keep me hospitalized for further observation, despite the *prima facie* evidence of my healed chest. I disappointed him, however, and checked out around five hours after Nadler and Ragma had departed. Hal picked me up and drove me home.

Declining an offer to dine with Hal and Mary, I retired early that evening, first calling Ginny, who now seemed anxious to resume life where we had been interrupted at it back in my undergraduate days. We made a date for the following afternoon, and I turned in after a brief constitutional about the neighborhood rooftops.

Troubled, my sleep? Yes. External security there was, to the extent of a pair of drowsy coplike stakeouts I had spotted from above while taking the air. Inside, though, I shuffled my deck of distresses and dealt myself bad hand after bad hand until I was cleaned out, mercifully, before six bells.

From then to morning was nine hours long for me and interspersed with short features, none of which I could get a pin through afterward, save for the smile. I awoke knowing what I had to do and immediately set about rationalizing it so that it would not seem like another compulsion. And after a time I decided that perhaps it was not. Really, anyone would be curious about the place where he almost died.

So I phoned Hal and tried to borrow his car. Mary was using it, though. However, Ralph's was available and I hiked over and picked it up.

It was a crisp, clear morning with a hint of balminess to come. Driving seaward, I thought of my new job and of Ginny and of the smile. The job was to outlast the current difficulty, Nadler had assured me, and the more I considered it the more it seemed that it might be worthwhile. If you have to do something, it is fortunate if it can be something interesting, something more than a little enjoyable. All those races out there, somewhere, concerning which we now knew next to nothing—I was going to have an opportunity to mine the unknown, hopefully to fetch forth something of understanding, to consider the exotic, to transform the familiar. I realized, suddenly, that I was excited at the prospect. I wanted to do it. I had no illusions as to why I had been hired, but now that I had my foot between door and jamb I wanted to push by the present obstructions and have a go at the real work. It seemed, just then, that alien anthropology (well, xenology, more correctly, I suppose) was really the sort of thing for which I had been preparing myself all along, in my own eclectic way. I chuckled softly. In addition to being excited, it occurred to me that I might be happy.

Having grown a bit more used to doing things in reverse, I found that driving a stereoisocar was not all that difficult. I came to a proper halt at every ꟼOTꙄ sign, and once I got out into the country there were very few traffic distractions. In fact, the only thing that had given me any trouble at all since the reversal was shaving. My traumatized nervous system had responded to the imaged reversal of a front-back reversal by jittering my hand to a bloody halt and waiting for me to dust off the electric shaver. This done, it was still a peculiar experience, but with the removal of the hazard it repaid me with confidence and a reasonably clean face.

And as I grinned and grimaced in the glass, I had thought of the only fragment of the night's dreaming that remained with me. There was this smile. Whose? I did not know. It was just a smile, somewhere a little over the line from the place where things begin to make sense. It remained with me, though, flickering on and off like a fluorescent tube about to call it quits; and as I drove along the route Hal had taken earlier, I tried free-associating my way around it, Doctor Marko not being handy.

Nothing but the "Mona Lisa" came to pass. It did not feel quite right, in terms of analytic correspondence. Still, it was this famous painting that had gone out in exchange for the Rhennius machine. There could be some subtle connection—at least in my subconscious—or else a red herring born of coincidence and imagination, which sounds more like a caption for a Dali or an Ernst than a Da Vinci.

I shook my head and watched the morning go by. After a time I came to the side road and took it.

Leaving the car where we had parked before, I located the path and made my way down to the cottage. I observed it discreetly for a long while, saw no signs of life. Ragma had insisted that I seek to avoid troublesome situations, but this hardly seemed to qualify as one. I approached it from the rear, advancing on the window through which Paul must have entered. Yes. The latch was broken. Peering inside, I saw a small bedroom, quite empty. Circling the building then, I glanced in the other windows, saw that the place was indeed deserted. The fractured front door was nailed shut, so I returned to the rear and entered after the fashion of my former mentor and master rockmaker.

I made my way through the bedroom and on out the door from which Paul had emerged. In the front room the signs of our struggles were unobliterated. I wondered which of the dried bloodstains might be my own.

I glanced out the window. The sea was calmer, with more to it than was the case the last time I had passed this way. It lay cleaner scud lines on the beach, where no new doorways gaped that I could see. Turning away from it then, I studied the tackle and netting which had taken Paul so neatly where he stood, upsetting the balance of power and getting me punctured that day.

Some lines and a section of mesh were still snagged by a nail in one of the rafters, loosely leashing the junk on the floor below. To my right, a series of two-by-fours nailed between wall supports made a track up to that level.

I climbed it and crossed among the rafters, pausing every few paces to strike a light and examine the dustcoated wood.

On the opposite side of the disturbed area where the equipment had rested, I came across a trail of small wedge-shaped smudges, leading in from a crossbrace which in turn bore them from the top of the side frame itself. I descended then and searched the rest of the cottage quite thoroughly but came across nothing else that was of any interest. So I went back outside, smoked a cigarette while I thought about it, then headed back for the car.

Smiles. Ginny had many of them that afternoon, and we spent the rest of the day avoiding troublesome situations. She was more than a little surprised to learn that I had graduated and gotten a job. No matter. The day had fulfilled its promise, was balmy, stayed bright. We ambled about the campus and the town, laughing and touching a lot. Later, we wound up at a chamber-music recital, which for some forgotten reason seemed the perfect thing to do and was. We stopped at a nearby café afterward, then went on up to my place so that I could show her it was only normally disarrayed, among other things. Smiles.

And the following day was a variation on the same theme. The weather varied also, a bit of rain beginning in the afternoon. But that was all right, too. Made things seem cozier. Nice to be inside. Imagining a roaring fireplace across the room. Stuff like that. She had not noticed that I was reversed, and I made up such a lovely lie for my scar, involving initiation into a secret society within a tribe I had recently fielded, that I almost wished I had written it down. Alack! And more smiles.

About nine in the evening my phone shattered the idyll. My premonition equipment printed out a warning, but like a Low Flying Aircraft sign failed to suggest anything I could do about it. I roused myself and answered the thing, a sigh followed by a "Yes?"

"Fred?"

"That's right."

"This is Ted Nadler. A problem has come up."

"Like what?"

"Zeemeister and Buckler have escaped."

"From where? How?"

"They had been transferred to a prison hospital later on in the same day they w ere brought in. They just left it a few hours ago, as nearly as we can tell. As to how they went about it, nobody seems to know. They left nine unconscious employees—medical and security—behind them. The doctors think it was some sort of neurotropic gas that was used—at least, the victims are all responding to atropine. But when the director called me none of them had come out of it sufficiently to be able to say what had occurred."

"Too bad. But then, I guess we've seen the last of them for a time."

"What do you mean?"

"What did I just say? They are probably on their way out of the country. Kidnapping charges, attempted homicide charges—reasons like that."

"We can't chance it."

"What do *you* mean?"

"They just might head your way instead. So you had better send your girlfriend home and pack a suitcase. I will be picking you up in around half an hour."

"You can't do that!"

"Sorry, but I can, and that's an order. Your job now requires that you take a trip. So does your health, for that matter."

"All right. Where?"

"New York," he said.

And then *click*. Thus, the invasion of Eden.

I returned to Ginny.

"What was that?" she asked.

"I have some good news and some bad news."

"What's the good news?"

"We still have half an hour."

Actually, it took him more like an hour to get to my place, which gave me time to make a nasty, coldblooded decision of a sort I had never had to make before and to act on it.

Merimee answered on the sixth ring and recognized my voice.

"Yes," I said. "Listen, do you recall an offer you made the last time that we talked?"

"Yes, I do."

"I'd like to take you up on it," I said.

"Who?"

"Two of them. Their names are Zeemeister and Buckler—"

"Oh, Morty and Jamie! Sure."

"You know them?"

"Yes. Morty used to work for your uncle occasionally. When business was booming and we were swamped with orders, we sometimes had to hire on extra help. He was a fat little kid, eager to learn the trade. I never much liked him myself, but he had enthusiasm and certain aptitudes. After Al fired him, he began operations on his own and built up a fairly decent business. He acquired Jamie a couple years later, to deal with competitors and handle customer complaints. Jamie used to be a light-heavyweight boxer—a pretty good one—and he had lots of military experience. Deserted from three different armies—"

"Why did Uncle Al fire Zeemeister?"

"Oh, the man was dishonest. Who wants untrustworthy employees?"

"True. Well, they've come close to killing me twice now, and I have just learned they are loose again."

"I take it you do not know their present whereabouts?"

"That, unfortunately, is the case."

"Hmm. It makes things more difficult. Well, let us get at it from the other end. Where are you going to be for the next few days?"

"I should be heading for New York within the hour."

"Excellent! Where will you be staying?"

"I don't know yet."

"You are welcome to stay here again. In fact, it might facilitate—"

"You don't understand," I said. "I've graduated. Doctorate, in fact. Now I have a job. My boss is taking me to New York tonight. I don't know where he will be putting me up yet. I'll try to call you as soon as I get in."

"Okay. Congratulations on the job and the degree. When you make up your mind to do something, you really move fast—just like your uncle. I look forward to hearing the whole story soon. In the meantime, I will put out some feelers. Also, I think I can promise you a pleasant surprise before too long."

"Of what sort?"

"Now, it would not be a surprise if I told you, would it, dear boy? Trust me."

"Okay, here's trust," I said. "Thanks."

"Till later."

"Goodbye."

Thus, with premeditation and full intent, et cetera. No apologies. I was tired of being shot, and it is always a shame to waste any sort of gift certificate.

The hotel, as it turned out, was directly across the street from the same partly fleshed skeleton of a possible office building that I had used to gain access to the roof of the structure diagonally across the street—namely, the hall that housed the Rhennius machine.

I somehow doubted that this was a matter of pure coincidence. When I commented on it, though, Nadler did not reply. It was after midnight that we were checking in, and I had been with the man continually since he had picked me up.

Then: "I'm about out of cigarettes," I said as we approached the desk, first noting, of course, that there was no cigarette machine in sight.

"Good," he replied. "Filthy habit."

The girl at the desk was more sympathetic, however, and told me where I could find one on the mezzanine. I thanked her, got our room number, told Nadler I would be up in a minute and left him there.

Naturally, I headed immediately for the nearest phone, got hold of Merimee and told him where I was.

"Good. Consider it staked out," he said. "By the way, I believe that the customers are in town. One of my associates thinks she saw them earlier."

"That was quick."

"Accidental, too. Still . . . Be of good cheer. Sleep well. *Adieu.*"

"G'night."

I headed for the elevators, caught one to my floor and sought our room. Lacking a key, I knocked.

There was no response for a time. Then, just as I was about to knock again, Nadler's voice inquired, "Who is it?"

"Me. Cassidy," I said.

"Come on ahead. It's unlocked."

Trusting, preoccupied and a trifle tired, I turned the knob, pushed and entered. A mistake anyone could have made.

"Ted! What the hell is—" and by then a vine had snagged me by the leg and another was slipping about my shoulder—"it?" I inquired, going airborne.

I struggled, of course. Who wouldn't? But the thing raised me a good five feet into the air, shifting me into a horizontal position directly above its less than attractive self. It then proceeded to turn me upside down, so that my field of vision was dominated by its gray-green bulk, its tub of slime and its octopod members all awrithe. I had a hunch it meant me ill even before its leafy appendages came open like switchblades, showing me their moist, spiny and suspiciously ruddy insides.

I let out a bleat and tore at the vines. Then something that felt like a red-hot poker occurred behind my eyes and passed from side to side and back within my head. Stark terror poured forth, and I twisted convulsively within the living bonds.

Then came what seemed a sharp whistling noise, the stabbing sensation was gone from my cranium, the vines slackened, collapsed, and I fell, twisting, to the carpet, narrowly missing the bucket's rim. A bit of the slime slopped over onto me, and inert tentacles fell like holiday streamers about me. I moaned and reached over to rub my shoulder.

"He's hurt!" came a voice that I recognized as Ragma's.

I turned my head to receive the sympathy I heard rushing toward me on little furry feet and big shod ones.

However, Ragma in his dog suit and Nadler and Paul Byler in equally appropriate garb rushed past me, squatted about the tub and began ministering to the militant vegetable. I crawled off into a corner, where I regained my feet if not my composure. Then I began mouthing obscenities, which were ignored. Finally, I shrugged, wiped the slime from my sleeve, found a chair, lit a cigarette and watched the show.

They raised the limp members and manipulated them, massaged them. Ragma tore off into the next room and returned with what appeared to be an elaborate lamp, which he plugged into an outlet and focussed on the nasty shrub. Producing an atomizer, he sprayed its vicious leaves. He stirred the slime. He dumped some chemicals into it.

"What could have gone wrong?" Nadler said.

"I have no idea," Ragma replied. "There! I think he is coming around!"

The tentacles began to twitch, like shocked serpents. Then the leaves opened and closed, slowly. A series of shudders shook the thing. Finally, it reared itself upright once again, extended all its members, let them go slack, extended them again, relaxed again.

"That's better," Ragma said.

"Anybody care how I'm feeling?" I asked.

Ragma turned and glared at me.

"You!" he said. "Just what did you do to poor Doctor M'mrm'mlrr, anyway?"

"Come again? My hearing seems to have been affected."

"What did you do to Doctor M'mrm'mlrr?"

"Thank you. That *is* what I thought you said. Damned if I know. Who is Doctor Murmur?"

"M'mrm'mlrr," he corrected. "Doctor M'mrm'mlrr is the telepathic analyst I brought to examine you. We made a good connection and got him here ahead of schedule. Then the first thing you do when he tries to examine you is incapacitate him."

"That thing," I inquired, gesturing at the tub and its occupant, "is the telepath?"

"Not everyone is a member of the animal kingdom, as you define it," he said. "The doctor is a representative of a totally different line of life development than your own. Anything wrong with that? Are you prejudiced against plants or something?"

"My prejudice is against being seized, squeezed and waved about in the air."

"The doctor practices a technique known as assault therapy."

"Then he should make allowance for the occasional patient who is not a pacifist. I don't know what I did, but I am glad that I did it."

Ragma turned away, cocked his head as if studying a gramophone horn, then announced, "He is feeling better. He wishes to meditate for a time. We are to leave the light on. It should not be overlong."

The vines stirred, moved to bunch themselves near the special lamp. Doctor M'mrm'mlrr grew still.

"Why does he want to assault his patients?" I asked. "It seems somewhat counterproductive to the building up of a good practice."

Ragma sighed and turned my way again.

"He does not do it to alienate his patients," he said. "He does it to help them. I guess that it is asking too much to expect you to appreciate the centuries of subtle philosophizing his people have devoted to this sort of thing."

"Yes," I replied.

"The theory is that any primary emotion can be used as a mnemomolecular key. Its skilled induction provides a telepath of his species with access to all of an individual's life experiences with resonance in that area. Now, it has been found that fear is a significant component of the problems most of his patients bring to him. Therefore, by inducing a flight response and frustrating it, he is able to sustain the emotion and keep the patient within range of therapy simultaneously. That way, he can review the emotive field in a single session."

"Does he eat his mistakes?" I asked.

"He has no control over his ancestry," Ragma replied. "Do you brachiate?" Then: "Never mind," he said. "*You* do. I forgot."

I turned to Nadler, who had just approached, and Paul, who was standing nearby, smirking.

"I take it all this sounds proper to you," I said, addressing them both.

Paul shrugged and Nadler said, "If it gets the job done."

I sighed.

"I suppose you are right," I said. Then: "Paul, what are you doing here?"

"Fellow employee," he replied. "I was recruited around the same time as yourself. By the way, I am sorry about that day back at your place. It *was* a matter of life and death, you know. Mine."

"Forget it," I said. "In what capacity have they got you on the payroll?"

"He is our expert on the stone," Nadler said. "He knows more about it than any other man alive."

"You've given up on the crown jewels, then?" I asked.

Paul winced. He nodded.

"You know, then," he said. "Yes, it was a belated youthful *geste* that got out of hand. *Mea culpa.* We had not anticipated the involvement of criminals to this extent. After I recovered from their abuse, I realized the mistake we had made and set out to put things right. I told the UN people everything I knew. Had a hard time convincing them but finally did. They were decent enough not to have me locked away somewhere. Even filled me in a bit concerning your difficulties down home. But making a clean breast of it was still not enough for me. I wanted to help recover the thing. You had just returned to the States, and I figured that they would try for you again. So I decided to keep an eye on you till they did, then spike their guns on the spot. I got onto your trail at Hal's and followed you as far as the Village, but I lost you in a bar there. Didn't catch up with you again till you were back home. You know the rest."

"Yes. Another small mystery resolved. Then you were hired in the hospital, too?"

"Correct. Ted here said that if I was that concerned about the way things were going, I might as well save some wasted motion and get paid for it, too. On the books, though, I am an XT-mineralogist."

"It seems to me," I said, addressing all of them, "That my being brought here tonight represents more than the mere avoidance of a couple of thugs. I would guess that you have something else in mind, only just beginning with the telepathic probe."

"Nor would you be incorrect," said Ragma. "However, since it is all contingent on the results of the analysis, it would be an exercise in redundancy to detail the various hypotheses which may have to be discarded."

"In other words, you are not going to tell me?"

"That pretty well sums it up."

Before I could submit my resignation or comment on any of a number of likely subjects that had occurred to me, I was distracted by a movement from across the room. Doctor M'mrm'mlrr was stirring again.

We all watched as he raised his snaky appendages and began his setting-up exercises. Stretch, relax . . . Stretch, relax . . .

Two or three minutes of this—it was kind of hypnotic—and I realized that he was stalking me again, only with a much greater delicacy than he had previously employed.

I felt the touch again, within my head, as an unnatural stirring beneath my basal thoughts. Only this time there was no accompanying pain. It was just a sort of dizzy feeling and a sense of process not unlike the awareness of something being done under a local anesthetic. I guess that the others had somehow been made aware of this also, for they maintained their positions and their silence.

All right. If M'mrm'mlrr was going to be a little more civilized about it, he could have my cooperation, I decided.

So I sat there and let him rummage about.

Then, quite abruptly, he must have come across the big switchboard somewhere down there and pulled a plug, because I blacked out, instantly and without pain. Blink.

Blink again.

Weary, thirsty and with a feeling of having been broken down and reconstituted incorrectly, I raised my hand to rub my eyes and glimpsed the face of my watch as I did so. Then I swung it up and listened for ticks. As I already suspected, it was still tossing them off. Ergo . . .

"Yes, about three hours," said Ragma.

I heard Paul snore, snort short, cough and sigh. He had been dozing in the armchair. Ragma was sprawled on the floor, smoking. M'mrm'mlrr was still upright and stirring. Nadler was nowhere in sight.

I stretched, unkinking muscle after muscle, hearing my frame creak like a floor that has been walked on overmuch.

"Well, I hope that you learned something useful," I said.

"Yes, I would say that we have," Ragma replied. "How do you feel?"

"Wrung out."

"Understandable. Yes. Very. You were something of a battle-ground for a while there."

"Tell me about it."

"To begin with," he said, "we have located the star-stone."

"Then you were right? Everyone was? I had the knowledge—somewhere?"

"Yes. The memory should even be accessible now. Want to try for it yourself? A party. A broken glass. The desk . . ."

"Wait a minute. Let me think."

I thought. And it was there. The last time that I had seen the star-stone . . .

It was the bachelor party I had given for Hal the week before his wedding. The apartment was crowded with our friends, the booze flowed, we made a lot of noise. It went on till around two or three in the morning. All in all I would have to say that it was an effective party. At least, it seemed that everyone went home laughing and there were no injuries.

Except for one small accident of my own.

Yes. A glass was elbowed off a side table, shattered. It was empty, though. Nothing to mop up. And it was right near the end of things. People were saying good night, leaving. So I left the pieces where they had fallen. Later. Mañana maybe.

Still, I knew that I had had too much to drink, could guess how I would feel the next morning and what I would doubtless do.

I would growl and curse and bid the day depart. When it persisted, I would roll out of bed, stagger off to the kitchen to put the coffee on—my first act on any day—then lumber back to the bathroom for standard maintenance while it brewed. Invariably barefoot. Certainly not remembering that my path was strewn with shards. At least for a brief while I would not remember. So I fetched the wastebasket from beneath the desk, got down into a hunker and began policing the area.

Naturally, I cut myself. I leaned too far forward at one point, lost my balance, extended a hand to maintain it and located another shard as my palm struck the floor.

I began bleeding, but I wrapped my handkerchief around it and continued with the cleanup. I knew that if I stopped right then to take care of my hand I would be tempted to let things go afterward. I was very sleepy.

So I got up all the pieces that I could see and wiped over the area with damp cocktail napkins. That done, I returned the wastebasket to its usual spot and dropped back into the desk chair because it was right there and I wanted to.

I unwrapped my hand and it was still bleeding. No sense doing anything at all until my thrombin earned its keep. So I leaned back and waited. My eyes did rest for a moment on the model of the star-stone we used for a paperweight. In fact, I reached out and turned it slowly, deriving a certain semisober satisfaction from the shifting light patterns it displayed. Then

I stretched out my arm full length on the blotter because my head was heavy and it occurred to me that my biceps would do nicely for a pillow. Resting that way, eyes still open, I continued to play with the stone, feeling a small regret at having gotten blood on it, then deciding that it was all right, as it made for amusing contrasts here and there. Goodbye, world.

It was a couple of hours later that I awoke, thirsty and possessed of a few muscle aches from the way I had been sleeping. I got to my feet, headed for the kitchen, where I drank a glass of water, then passed back through the apartment, switching off lights. When I got to my bedroom, I undressed slowly, sitting on the edge of the bed, letting my clothes lie where they fell, crawled in and did the rest of my night's sleeping properly.

And that was the last time I had seen the star-stone. Yes.

"I remember," I said. "I have to hand it to the doctor. It comes back now. It was misted over by booze and fatigue, but I've got it again."

"Not just beverage and fatigue," Ragma said.

"What else, then?"

"I said that we had found the stone."

"Yes, you did. But no memories on that count have been shaken loose for me. I just recall the last time that I saw it, not where it went."

Paul cleared his throat. Ragma glanced at him.

"Go ahead," he said.

"When I worked with that thing," Paul told me, "I had to proceed along lines that were somewhat less than satisfactory. I mean that I was not about to knock a piece off a priceless artifact for purposes of analysis. Aside from purely aesthetic reasons, it might be detected. I had no idea as to how detailed any alien analyses of its surface might be. Almost anything I did that would alter it might have caused trouble. Fortunately, though, it passed light readily. So I concentrated on its optical effects. I did an extremely minute topological light-mapping of its entire surface. With that and its weight, I developed some ideas as to its composition. Now, although I was not especially concerned at the time with anything other than duplicating it, it did strike me that the thing seemed like a mass of strangely crystallized protein—"

"I'll be damned," I said. "But . . ."

I looked at Ragma.

"Organic, all right," he said. "Paul did not really discover anything new in that, as this fact had been known for some time elsewhere. However, what nobody had realized was that it was still living, somehow. It was simply dormant."

"Living? Crystallized? You make it sound like a massive virus."

"I suppose that I do. But viruses are not noted for their intelligence, and that thing—in its own way—is intelligent."

"I do see what you are leading up to, of course," I said. "What do I do now? Reason with it? Or take two aspirins and go to bed?"

"Neither. I am going to have to speak for Doctor M'mrm'mlrr now, as he is occupied and you deserve an immediate explanation as to what he discovered. The first time that he attempted to penetrate your memories, he was thrown into a state of shock by an encounter with a totally unexpected form of consciousness coexistent with your own. In the course of his practice he has treated representatives of just about every known race in the galaxy, but he never encountered anything like this before. He said that it was something unnatural."

"Unnatural? In what way?"

"In a strictly technical fashion. He believes it to be an artificial intelligence, a synthetic being. Such things have been produced by a number of our contemporaries, but all of them are fairly simple compared to this."

"What functions does mine perform?"

"We do not know. The second time that M'mrm'mlrr entered your mind, he was braced for the encounter. The creature is itself mildly telepathic, you see. Enough to translate for you back aboard our ship, under ideal conditions. I am told that this can provide additional complications, and apparently it did. However, he succeeded in subduing it and learned sufficient of its nature in the process so that we have an idea as to how to deal with it. He then went on to explore some of your memories touching on the phenomenon, which helped us piece together our line of attack. He is now occupied in holding the creature in a form of mental stasis until things are ready."

"Things? Ready? What things? How?"

"We should be hearing shortly. It is all tied in, though, with the nature of the thing. In light of M'mrm'mlrr's findings, Paul has worked out some ideas as to what happened and what can be done about it."

Paul took the pause that followed as a cue and said, "Yes. Picture it this way: You have a synthetic life form that can apparently be switched on and off by means of isometric reversals. Its 'on' condition, characterized by life functions, is a product of left-handedness. This, as you know, is the normal form amino acids take here on Earth, also; L-amino acids, as they are called. Turn them into their stereoisomer—D-amino acids—and in the case of our specimen, it goes into the 'off' position. Now, when I examined the star-stone, the optical effects indicated the dextral situation. 'Off.' All right. I was not thinking along these lines, but now we know a lot more. We know you were drinking the night you got blood on it. We know that grain alcohol has a symmetrical molecule and that if it could react with the specimen in one isometric state it might do it in the other also. Either it is a flaw in its design or an intentionally engineered capability. This we do not know. M'mrm'mlrr learned that it did its best communicating with you, however, in the presence of this molecule—so it does seem to stimulate conversation. Whatever, you excited it sufficiently to enable it to partially activate itself and enter your system by way of the incision in your hand. After this exertion, it lay dormant for a long while, as you are not much of a drinker. Every now and then it gained a little stimulation, though, and tried to contact you via one sensory route or another. The medication Ragma administered to you after Australia revived it somewhat as it involved some ethyl alcohol. The night you were drinking with Hal, however, was the breakthrough. If it could persuade you to reverse yourself by means of the Rhennius machine, you would of course be backward, but it would be switched on. Which is what happened. So it is functioning normally at present, in you, but your health is suffering, according to Ragma. What we have to do now is get it out of you and rereverse you."

"Can you?"

"We think so."

"But you still have no idea what it does?"

"It is a very sophisticated living machine of unknown function that conned you into placing yourself in a dangerous situation. Also, it displays a predilection for mathematics."

"Some sort of computer, then?"

"M'mrm'mlrr does not think so. He believes it to be a secondary function."

"I wonder why it didn't get back in touch with me after it was switched on?"

"There was still the barrier."

"What barrier?"

"The matter of stereoisomers. Only this time it was you who were reversed. Then, too, it had gotten what it wanted."

"Give it its due," said Ragma. "It did do one thing for him."

"What was that?" I asked.

"I did not do anything for you back at the hospital," he said. "When I removed the dressing and performed a number of tests, I found that you were already completely healed. Your parasite apparently took care of it."

"Then it seems as if he is trying to be a benign little guy."

"Well, if anything should happen to you . . ."

"Granted, granted. But what about the side effects of the reversal on me?"

"I am not at all certain that he realizes what it could eventually lead to."

"It seems strange that if he is intelligent and he and M'mrm'mlrr were in contact he did not offer any explanation as to what has been going on."

"There was small time for amenities," Ragma said. "The doctor had to act quickly to freeze him."

"More of his assault philosophy? It hardly seems fair—"

The telephone rang. Paul answered it, and all of his responses were monosyllables. It lasted perhaps half a minute and then he hung up and turned to Ragma.

"Ready," he said.

"All right," Ragma replied.

"What is ready?" I asked.

"That was Ted," Paul told me. "He is across the street. He had to get authorization—and the key—to open up the place. We are all going over now."

"To reverse me?"

"Right," said Ragma.

"Do you know how to do it?" I asked. "That machine has several settings. I tested its program once, and I have a great respect for the variations it can toss off."

"Charv will be meeting us there," he replied, "and he is bringing along a copy of the operator's manual."

Paul moved off into the bedroom, returned pushing a pad-
ded cart.

"Give me a hand with the leafy bloke, will you, Fred?" he
said.

"Sure."

It was with very mixed feelings that I moved forward and did
so, taking care the while not to get any more of the slop on me.

As we pushed Doctor M'mrm'mlrr through the lobby and
out onto the sidewalk, the reflection of a neon sign seemed, in
the after-image of a blinking, to read DO YOU SMELL ME
DED?

"Yes," I muttered under my breath. "Tell me what to do."

"Our Snark is a Boojum," came a whisper as we were cross-
ing the street.

When I looked around, of course, there was no one there.

11

I FELT NO REAL CHANGE with the disengagement that Ragma told me was taking place. I kept my eyes firmly fixed on Charv, who was going round and round, fiddling with the Rhennius machine, with frequent reference to a manual he carried in his pouch. It was not that I was squeamish. Well, maybe it was.

The incision in my left arm stung a bit but was not especially painful. Ragma had wanted to avoid the introduction of additional chemicals of unknown effect to the area, which was understandable, and I was partially successful in setting up a biofeedback block. So my bared left arm rested on a previously white hotel towel, which I was brightening and darkening here and there beneath the area where he had swabbed alcohol, slashed me and applied more alcohol. I was resting in a swivel chair belonging to one of the guards we had relieved, trying not to think about the eviction of the star-stone from my premises. It was taking place, all right. I could tell that from the expressions on Paul's and Nadler's faces.

Situated right beside the base of the Rhennius machine, M'mrm'mlrr swayed and concentrated—or whatever he did— to cause what was taking place to take place. A bit of moon showed through the skylight. The hall echoed the least sound and was cold as a tomb.

I was not really certain that what was being done was the right thing. On the other hand, I could not be sure that it was not. It was not the same thing as doublecrossing a friend or betraying a confidence, or anything like that, both because my guest had been of the uninvited variety and because I had given him what he was after—*viz.*, namely & to wit, I had turned him on.

Still, though, echoing up from the chambers of my memory came the thought that he had given me the legal citation I had needed back when I was searching for something to keep them from spiriting me away. And he had put my chest together again. And he had promised to clarify everything, eventually.

But my metabolism meant a lot to me, and that spell on the bus and my experience of being controlled back in the hospital were also distressing. I had made my decision. Second thoughts were now a waste of time and emotion. I waited.

Our Snark is a Boojum!

There it was again, desperate-sounding this time, followed by the superimposition of massive teeth framed by upward curving lips on the far wall. Then fading, fading . . . Gone.

"We have him!" said Ragma, slapping a pad of gauze onto my arm. "Hold that in place for a while."

"Right."

It was only then that I ventured a look.

The star-stone was there on the towel. Not quite as I remembered it, for its shape was somewhat altered and its colors seemed more vivid—near to pulsing.

Our Snark is a Boojum. Anything from a distorted appeal for reconsideration to a euphemistic warning to a wasp concerning certain flowers—distorted as it was by the handedness barrier. I would have given a lot just then to know, though.

"What are you going to do with it now?" I asked.

"Get it to a safe place," Ragma said, "after you've taken your little turnabout. Then it will be up to your United Nations for a time, since they are its current custodians. Still, a report on this new finding will have to be circulated among all our member worlds, and I would imagine your authorities will want to act under their advisement as to tests and observations that might now be in order."

"I'd imagine," I said, and he reached to pick it up.

"There's a good little fellow" came an all too familiar voice from across the hall. "Gingerly, gingerly now! Wrap it in the towel, please. I'd hate to have it chipped or scratched."

Zeemeister and Buckler had entered the hall, carrying guns, pointing them. Jamie, who was grinning, remained near the entrance, covering it. Morton, who looked pretty pleased himself, advanced on us.

"So that's how you hid it, Fred," he observed. "Neat trick."

I said nothing but rose slowly to my feet, nothing in mind but the fact that I could move faster from that position.

He shook his head.

"No need for trouble," he said. "This time you are safe, Fred. Everyone here is safe. So long as I get the stone."

I wondered, in a hopefully telepathic fashion, whether M'mrm'mlrr might reach out and burn his brain as a contribution to domestic tranquillity.

The suggestion was apparently accepted just as he came up beside me and hefted the stone. For he shrieked then and suffered a minor convulsion.

I grabbed for the gun with both hands. Jamie was far enough away to give me sporting odds on the attempt. I did not think he would take a chance on hitting his boss.

The pistol was fired twice before I tore it away from him. I did not get to keep it, however, as he jabbed me in the belly and caught me with an uppercut that knocked me to the floor. The weapon went spinning and skidding away to a place somewhere beneath the platform of the Rhennius machine.

Zeemeister kicked Ragma, who had chosen that moment to attack, away from him. Still clutching the stone, he produced a long, shiny blade from somewhere in the vicinity of his forearm. Then he shouted to Jamie but stopped in mid-cry.

I looked to see what had happened and decided that it must be another hallucination.

Jamie's weapon lay half a dozen paces behind him, and he stood rubbing his wrist, facing the man with the neat beard and the amused expression, the man who held one hand in his pocket and twirled a shillelagh with the other.

"I'll kill you," I heard Jamie say.

"No, Jamie! No!" Zeemeister cried. "Don't go near him, Jamie! Run!"

Zeemeister backed away, pausing only to slash one of M'mrm'mlrr's tentacles, as if knowing the source of his mental anguish.

"He's not much," Jamie called back.

"That's Captain Al!" Zeemeister shouted. "Run, you fool!"

But Jamie decided to swing instead.

It was instructive to almost behold. "Almost," I say, because the cudgel moved a bit too fast for me to trace its passage. So I was not certain exactly where or how many times it touched him. It seemed only an instant after Jamie began his swing that he was falling.

Then, still twirling the stick, casually, Jauntily now, the hallucination moved past Jamie's crumpled form and headed on toward Zeemeister.

Not taking his eyes from the advancing figure, Zeemeister continued to retreat, holding the knife low before him, edge upward.

"I thought you were dead," he finally said.

"Obviously you were mistaken" came the reply.

"What interest have you in this thing, anyway?"

"You tried to kill Fred Cassidy," he said, "and I've invested a lot in that boy's education."

"I did not associate the name," Zeemeister replied. "But I never really intended to harm him."

"That is not the way that I heard it."

Zeemeister continued to back away, passing through the gate in the guardrail, moving until the rotating platform of the Rhennius machine brushed the backs of his pant legs. He spun then and slashed at Charv, who was passing by, brandishing a wrench. Charv bleated and fled the platform, dropping to the floor near M'mrm'mlrr and Nadler.

"What are you going to do, Al?" Zeemeister inquired, turning back to face the other.

But there was no reply, only a continued advance, a continued twirling of the club, a smile.

At the last instant, before he came into shillelagh range, Zeemeister bolted. Raising one foot to the platform, he sprang back on it, turning, and rushed forward all of two paces. Its rotation, however, had so positioned the apparatus that he collided with the central unit, which faintly resembled a wide hand cupped as in the act of scratching.

His momentum and angle of incidence were such that his stumbling rebound bore him down atop the belt. His knife and the towel-swathed star-stone flew from his hands as he tried to stay his fall. They bounced from the platform down onto the floor as he was borne on into the tunnel. His scream was cut short with an ominous abruptness and I looked away, but not in time.

It apparently turned him inside out.

Which of course delivered the contents of his circulatory and digestive systems to the floor.

Also, it seemed to have inverted all of the organs which were now exposed.

The contents of my own stomach sought egress, reinforced by the noises which had begun about me. Like I said, I looked away. But not in time.

It was Charv who finally managed to get up stomach enough to get to them and throw someone's coat over the remains, where they had fallen from the belt as it advanced toward the perpendicular. Then, and only then, did Ragma's practicality return, punctuated by his near hysterical "The stone! Where is the stone?"

Through watering eyes, I sought for it and then beheld the racing form of Paul Byler, bloody towel clutched beneath his arm, on his way across the hall.

"Once a jolly swagman," he called out, "always a jolly swagman!" and he was gone out the door.

Pandemonium reigned. Over the just and the near just.

My hallucination then gave a final spin to his stick, turned, nodded in my direction and approached us. I rose to my feet, nodded back, found a smile and showed it to him.

"Fred, my boy, you've grown," he said. "I hear you have acquired a high degree and a responsible position. Congratulations!"

"Thank you," I said.

"How are you feeling?"

"Rather like Pip," I told him, "though my expectations are simple things, I never realized what your export-import business was actually all about."

He chuckled. He embraced me.

"Tut, lad. Tut," he said, pushing me back to arm's length again. "Let me look at you. There. So that's how you turned out, is it? Could be worse, could be worse."

"Byler has the stone!" Charv shrieked.

"The man who just left—" I began.

"—shan't get very far, lad. Frenchy is outside to prevent anyone's departing this place with unseemly haste. In fact, if you listen you may hear the clatter of hooves on marble."

I did, and I did. I also heard profanity and the sounds of a struggle without.

"Who, sir, are you?" Ragma inquired, rising up onto his hind legs and drawing near.

"This is my Uncle Albert," I said, "the man who put me through school: Albert Cassidy."

Uncle Albert studied Ragma through narrowed eyes as I explained, "This is Ragma. He is an alien cop in disguise. His partner is named Charv. He is the kangaroo."

Uncle Al nodded.

"The art of disguise has come a long way," he observed. "How do you manage the effect?"

"We are *extraterrestrial* aliens," Ragma explained.

"Oh, that does make a difference then. You will have to excuse my ignorance of these matters. For a number of years and a variety of reasons have I been a man whose very blood is snow-broth, numb to the wanton stings and motions of the senses. Are you a friend of Fred's?"

"I have tried to be," Ragma replied.

"It is good to know that," he said, smiling. "For, extraterrestrial alien or no, if you were here to harm him, not all the cheese in Cheshire would buy your safety. Fred, what of these others?"

But I did not answer him because I had chosen that moment to glance upward, had seen something just as he had spoken and was in the process of having the *1812 Overture,* smoke signals, semaphores and assorted fireworks displays simultaneously active within my head.

"The smile!" I cried and tore off toward the rear of the hall.

I had never been past the door at that end of the place, but I was familiar with the reversed layout of the roof and that was all that I needed to know just then.

I plunged through and followed the corridor that lay behind. When it branched, I headed to the left. Ten quick paces, another turn and I saw the stairway off to the right. Reaching it, I swung around the rail post and took the steps two at a time.

How it all fit I did not know. But that it did I did not doubt.

I reached a landing, took a turn, came to another, took another. The end of things came into view.

There was a final landing with a door at the head of the stairs, all enclosed in a kiosk with small, meshed windows about. I hoped that the door opened from the inside without a key—it looked like that sort of handle arrangement—because it would take a while to smash through a window and its grillwork, if I could do it at all. As I ascended, I cast my eyes about, looking for tools for this purpose.

I spotted some junk that might serve that end, as no one had apparently envisioned anyone wanting to break out of the place. It proved unnecessary, however, for the door yielded when I depressed the handle and threw my weight against it.

It was of the heavy, slow-opening sort, but when I had finally thrust it aside and stepped out I was certain that I was near to something important. I blinked against the darkness, trying to sort pipes, stacks, hatch covers and shadows into the notches my memory provided. Somewhere among them all, beneath the stars, the moon and the Manhattan skyline, was one special slot that I had to fill. The odds might be against it, but I had moved quickly. If the entire guess held true, there was a chance
. . .

Catching my breath, I studied the panorama. I circled the kiosk slowly, my back to it, staring outward, scrutinizing every dark patch and cranny on the roof, on the ledges, beyond. It was almost a literally proverbial situation, only this was not a coal cellar and it was past midnight.

The object of my search might seem to have several advantages. Along with a growing certainty that I was right, however, I had persistence. I would not go away. I would outwait him if he were waiting. I would pursue him if I glimpsed his flight.

"I know you are there," I said, "and I know that you can hear me. There must be an accounting now, for we have been pushed too far. I have come for it. Will you surrender yourself and answer our questions? Or do you wish to make a bad situation worse by being difficult about it?"

There came no answer. I still had not caught sight of what I had hoped to find.

"Well?" I said. "I am waiting. I can wait as long as is necessary. You have to be breaking the law—*your* law. I am positive of that. The nature of the entire setup requires injunctions against activities of this sort. I have no idea as to your motives, but they are not especially material at this point. I suppose that I should have caught on sooner, but I did not extend my recent awareness of the diversity of alien life forms quite quickly enough. So you got away with a lot. Back at the shack? Yes, I guess that is where I should have made the connection, the second time around. There were a few earlier encounters, but I think I may be excused missing their significance. Right here even, the night I tested the machine . . . Are you ready to come out? No? All right. My guess is that you are telepathic and that all these words are unnecessary, as I did not hear you say anything to Zeemeister. Still, I am not of a mind to settle for anything less than certainty, so I shall continue in this fashion. I believe you possess a tapetum, like your model. I saw the light from below. Keep your eyes closed or your head turned away, or I'll spot the light. Then, of course, you will not be able to see me. Your telepathic sense, though? I wonder now. It just occurred to me that you might betray yourself to M'mrm'mlrr if you use it. He isn't all that far away. It is possible that you are now at a disadvantage. What do you say? Do you want to be graceful about it? Or would you rather sit out a long siege?"

Still nothing. But I refused to let a doubt enter my mind.

"Stubborn, aren't you?" I went on. "But then I would imagine you have a lot to lose. Ragma and Charv seem to have a bit of leeway in their work, though, being this far from the center of things. Perhaps they know some way to make it go a trifle easier for you. I don't know. Just talking. Worth thinking about, though. I believe the fact that no one has followed me up here indicates that M'mrm'mlrr is reading my thoughts and reporting the situation below. They must already be aware of everything that I have figured out. They must know that what tripped you up was no fault of your own. I do not believe that you or anyone else realized until just recently that the star-stone was sentient and that when I switched it on it began recording data, tabulating it, processing it. It had a rough time because of the handedness barrier which still persisted, though, because what turned it on pretty much turned me off—for purposes of communicating with it. So it could not simply come out and deliver its conclusions concerning yourself. It gave me a line from Lewis Carroll, though. Maybe it picked it up back in the bookstore. I don't know. It has had twisted versions of all my memories to play with, too. Wherever it got it, it did not click for me. Even though it was the second such attempt. The smile came first. Nothing there for me either. Not until Uncle Albert said 'Cheshire' and I looked up and saw the outline of a cat against the moon, above the skylight. You dumped all that fishing gear on Paul Byler. Zeemeister was your creature. You needed human agents, and he was the perfect choice: venal, criminally competent and knowledgeable of the situation from the beginning. You bought him and sent him after the stone.

Only the stone had other ideas, and at the last minute I caught them. You are in the form of a black cat who has crossed my path one time too many. Now I am thinking that if there are any lights up here, someone down below ought to go looking for the switchbox. Maybe they are already on their way to it. Shall we go below or wait for them? I'll nail you once they come on."

Despite the fact that I thought myself prepared for anything, I was taken by surprise in the next instant. I screamed when it hit, and I tried to protect my eyes. What a fool I had been!

I had looked everywhere but on top of the kiosk.

Claws dug into my scalp, scratched at my face. I tore at the creature but could not get a hold that would dislodge it. Desperately, then, I threw my head back toward the wall of the kiosk.

Predictably—by hindsight—it leaped away just as I did this and I brained myself against the wall.

Cursing, staggering, holding my head, I was unable for the moment to pursue the thing. Several moments, in fact . . .

Straightening finally, wiping the blood from my forehead and cheeks, I looked for it again. This time I caught the movement. It was bounding toward the edge of the roof, it was up onto the low guard wall . . .

It paused there. It glanced back. Mocking me? I caught the flash from those eyes.

"You've had it," I said, and started forward.

It turned and raced along the wall then. Too fast, it seemed, to be able to stop when it reached the corner.

Nor did it.

I did not think it would make it, but I had underestimated its strength.

The lights came on just as it sprang into the air, and I had a full view of the black cat shape, sailing, forelimbs extended, far

196

out beyond the edge of the building. Then descending, dropping from view—no nine lives to fool with either, I felt sure—followed by a soft impact, a scratching, a clicking.

Racing forward, I saw that it had made it across. It was onto the skeleton of the building that stood beside the hall, onto it and already retreating across a girder.

I did not break my stride.

I had taken an easier way across that night I had last visited the roof, but there was no time for such luxury now—at least, that was how I had rationalized it after the fact. Actually, I suppose, those impetuous spinal nerves should have the credit this time, too. Or the blame.

I estimated the jump automatically as I approached, leaped from what my body told me was precisely the proper spot, cleared the guard wall, kept my eyes on my target and my arms ready.

I always worry about my shins on something like this. One bad bash to them and the pain could be sufficient to break the chain of necessary actions. And a close bit of coordination was required here—another bad feature. An ideal climbing situation involves one key action at a time. Two can still be okay. Too much to coordinate, though, and you get into the foolish risk area. At any other time this one would be foolish. I seldom jump for handholds. If there is an alternative save, I may. But that is about all. I'm not one for the all-or-nothing feat. However . . .

My feet struck the girder with a jolt I felt in my wisdom teeth. My left arm hooked about the upright I-beam beside which I had landed, things of which Torquemada would have approved occurring within my shoulder. I fell forward then but was simultaneously swung leftward as I lost my footing, thrusting my right arm across and around to catch hold of the same upright. Then I drew myself back onto the girder, caught my balance and held it. I released my hold on the upright as I sighted my quarry.

It was heading for the platformed section where the workmen kept their things in barrels and tarp-covered heaps. I started for that place myself, running along girders, plotting the shortest route, ducking and sidestepping where necessary.

It saw me coming. It mounted a heap, a crate, sprang to the floor above. I took hold of a strut and the side of a beam, swung myself up, found purchase for my left foot at the head of the strut, raised myself, caught hold of the girder overhead, pulled myself up.

As I came to my feet, I saw it vanishing over the edge of the platform on the next floor above. I repeated my climb.

It was nowhere in sight. I could only assume that it had continued on upward. I followed.

Three floors above that I glimpsed it again. It had paused to peer down at me from a narrow width of planking that served as an elevator landing for workmen. The light from below and behind caught its eyes once more.

Then movement!

I clung to my support and raised an arm to shield my head. But this proved unnecessary.

The clatter and the bouncing, pinging, ringing that spilled from the bucket of bolts or rivets it had pushed over the edge came to me, passed by me, echoed on down to the ground, where it ended/ended/finally ended.

I saved the breath I might have used on curses for purposes of climbing and resumed my vertical trek once more as soon as the air was clear. A cold wind began to tug at me as I went. Glancing back and down, I saw figures on the still-illuminated rooftop next door, looking upward. How much they could see I was not certain.

By the time I reached the place from which the flak had fallen, the subject of my pursuit was two floors higher and apparently catching its breath. It was easier for me to see now, as the platforms had dwindled down to a precious few bits of planking and we were coming into a realm of hard, straight lines and cold, clean angles as classic and spare as a theorem out of Euclid.

The winds pushed and pulled with a bit more force as I mounted higher, slowly surrendering their randomness and growing constant. Starting at my fingertips and entering into the rest of me came a sense of the slight arrhythmic swaying that possessed the structure. The sleep sounds of the city grew indistinguishable in terms of isolated noises. It was a snoring, then a humming and finally the winds ate it and digested it. The stars and the moon traced the geometry through which we maneuvered and all the surfaces were dry, which is really about all that a night climber can ask for.

I kept on after it, up. Up. Up the two levels that separated us. Then one more.

It stood one level above me then, glaring down. There were no more stories. This was as high as things had gotten. And so it waited.

I paused and glared back.

"Ready to call it quits?" I shouted. "Or do we play it out all the way?"

There was no answer. No movement either. It just stood there and watched me.

I ran my hand upward along the beam that rose beside me.

My quarry grew smaller. It had crouched, bunched up, tensed itself. As if to spring . . .

Damn it! I would be at a disadvantage for several moments when I reached that level. My head exposed, my arms and hands occupied as I drew myself up.

Yet, it would be taking quite a chance itself, springing at me, up there, bringing itself into range.

"I think you are bluffing," I said. "I'm coming up."

I tightened my grip on the upright.

A thought came into my mind then, of the sort that seldom entered there: *What if you fall?*

I hesitated—it was such a novel notion—an idea one simply does not entertain. Of course I was aware that it could occur. It had happened to me a number of times, with varying results. It is not the sort of thing one dwells on to the point of preoccupation, however.

Still, it is a long way down. Do you ever wonder what your final thought will be, just before the lights go out?

I suppose that everyone has, at some time or other, for a moment or so. It is hardly worth prolonged cerebration, however, and would probably be classifiable as a symptom of something that ought to be sacrificed on the smudgy altar of mental health. But . . .

Look down. How far? How great a distance? What does it feel like to fall? Is there a tingling in your wrists, hands, feet, ankles?

Of course. But again—

Vertigo! It swept over me. Wave upon wave. A thing I had never before experienced with such intensity.

Simultaneously, I realized the unnatural source of my discomfort. It would require a superfluity of naïveté not to.

My furry little enemy was broadcasting the sensation, trying to create an acrophobic attitude, succeeding.

But some things must go beyond the physical, the somatopsychic. At least, those small shreds of mysticism which make up the only religion I know kept insisting it wasn't all that simple to turn love into hate, passion to fear, to overcome the will of a lifetime with the irrationality of a moment.

I beat my fist against the beam, I gnawed at my lip. I was scared. Me. Fred Cassidy. Scared to climb it.

Falling, falling . . . Not the drifting of a leaf or a stray bit of paper, but the plummeting of a heavy body . . . The only interference, perhaps, the bars of our cage. . . A bloody print here, there . . . That is the only statement you may record on your passage down . . . As from the trees where your not-so-distant ancestors clung, fearfully—

I saw it then. It had just given me what I needed, what I had been groping for while trying to bear the assault: an object outside myself on which I could focus my attention fully. It had allowed a patronizing attitude toward the whole human race to slip through just then. Sibla had irritated me with a touch of the same sentiment back at Merimee's place. It was all that I needed.

I allowed myself to get mad as hell. I encouraged it, stoked it.

"All right," I said. "Those same ancestors used to poke things like you off limbs just for laughs—to watch you spit and fall, to see whether you always landed on your feet. It's an old game. Hasn't been played properly in ages. I am about to revive it, in the name of my fathers. Behold the riant anthropoid, beware its crooked thumbs!"

I seized the beam and pulled myself up.

It backed up, paused, advanced, paused again. I felt a growing elation at its indecisiveness, a sense of triumph over the halting of the bombing of my mind. When I reached its level I ducked my head low and thrust both hands up onto the girder far enough apart so that whichever got clawed the other would still be sufficient for support.

It made as if to attack, apparently thought better of it, then turned and ran.

I pulled myself up. I stood.

I watched it scamper away, not halting until it was on the opposite side of the square of steel we held. Then I moved to the nearest corner and it moved to the farthest corner. I started up the next side. It started down the opposite side. I halted. It halted. We stared at each other.

"Okay," I said, taking out a cigarette and lighting it. "With a stalemate you lose, you know. Those folks below aren't just sitting on their hands. They're calling for assistance. Every route down will be covered before long. I'm betting someone will be by soon in a chopper, too—with a mercy gun with infrared sights. I have always understood it to be a little better thing to surrender than to resist arrest when you are in trouble. I am a bona fide representative of both my country's State Department and the United Nations. Choose whichever one you prefer. I—"

Very well, the thought came into my mind. *I will surrender to you in your capacity as a State Department employee.*

It immediately moved to the next corner, turned there and advanced along that side at a steady pace. I turned back, moving toward the corner I had recently quit. It reached that point before I did, however, turned and continued on toward me.

"Hold it right there," I said, "and consider yourself in custody."

Instead, it bounded forward and sprang toward me, my mind instantly filling with something which, when supplied with words, came through, roughly, as *It is*

$$
more \begin{Bmatrix} satisfying \\ noble \end{Bmatrix} to\ die\ with\ your \begin{Bmatrix} teeth \\ claws \end{Bmatrix} \begin{Bmatrix} in \\ at \end{Bmatrix} the
$$
$$
\begin{Bmatrix} throat \\ heart \end{Bmatrix} of\ the\ enemy\ of \begin{Bmatrix} nest \\ totem \\ civilization \end{Bmatrix} !\ Die,\ nest\text{-}
$$
molester!

My hand had shot forward just as it was springing, and for want of any other weapon I had flipped my cigarette into its face.

It twisted and slapped at it just before its feet left the girder. I tried to drop back and go into a crouch at the same time, raising my arms for balance, for protection.

It hit me, but not in the throat or heart. It struck against my left shoulder, clawing wildly, raking my left arm and side. And then it fell.

An instant of thoughts and actions inseparable: Regain my balance, save the nasty little thing—for whatever it knew—right arm crossbody, weight shift to left foot, left hand dipping, hooking, seizing—don't overcompensate!—comes now the jerk, the tugging, the pull—

I had it! I had hold of it by the tail! But—

A brief resistance, a sudden ripping, a new shifting of moment . . .

I held only a black, stiff, artificial tail, shreds of some rubbery costume material still attached. I caught a glimpse of the small, dark form as it passed through the area of greater illumination below. I don't believe that it landed on its feet.

12

TIME.

More fragments, pieces, bits . . . Time.

Epiphany in Black & Light, Scenario in Green, Gold, Purple & Gray . . .

There is a man. He is climbing in the dusky daysend air, climbing the high Tower of Cheslerei in a place called Ardel beside a sea with a name he cannot quite pronounce as yet. The sea is as dark as the juice of grapes, bubbling a Chianti and chiaroscuro fermentation of the light of distant stars and the bent rays of Canis Vibesper, its own primary, now but slightly beneath the horizon, rousing another continent, pursued by the breezes that depart the inland fields to weave their courses among the interconnected balconies, towers, walls and walkways of the city, bearing the smells of the warm land toward its older, colder companion . . .

Climbing from hold to green stone on the seaward side of the structure, he has contrived to race with the last of the day as it flees upward, tilts, prepares to jump. In the antic light of evening the top of the Tower of Cheslerei is the last spot touched by the day gold before its departure from the capitol. He has given himself the time from the beginning of sunset to race the final light from bottom to top, to be on hand to take the night as it comes into the last place.

He is racing with shadows now, his own already diffuse about him, his hands darting like fish above the darkness. In the great high places above him the night continues with the minting of stars. Through atmosphere's crystal mask, he glimpses their englossment as he goes. He is panting now, and the spot of gold has diminished. The shadows begin to pass him as he mounts.

But it lingers, that tiny touch of gold on the green. Thinking, perhaps, of another place of green and gold, he moves even faster, pacing his shadow, gaining on it. The light fades for an instant, returns for another.

During that instant, he catches hold of the parapet and heaves himself upward, like a swimmer departing the water.

He draws himself up and stands, turning his head toward the sea, toward the light. Yes . . .

He catches the final fleck of gold that it tosses. For a moment only he stares after it.

He seats himself then on the stone and regards the night's other thousands, as he had never seen them before. For a long while, he watches . . .

I know him well, of course.

Portrait of Boy & Dog Romping on the Beach, Tick-Tock and Tempest Past, Fragment—

"Fetch, boy! Fetch!"

"Damn it, Ragma! Learn to throw a frisbee properly if you want to play! I'm getting tired of going after it!"

He chuckled. I recovered it and sailed it back. He caught it and threw it, to lose it again in the bushes upshore.

"That's it," I said. "I quit. It's hopeless. You catch fine, but you throw lousy."

I turned and headed back toward the water. A few moments later I heard a scuffing noise and he was at my side.

"We have a game somewhat like that back home," he said. "I was never very good at it there either."

We watched the waves foam in, green to gray, crowding and frothing as they ran.

"Give me a cigarette," Ragma said.

I did, taking one myself also.

"If I tell you what I know you want to know, I will be breaking security," he said.

I said nothing. I had already guessed as much.

"But I am going to tell you anyhow," he went on. "Not details. Just the general picture. I am going to exercise my discretion. It is really pretty much an open secret, and now that your people are beginning to travel to other worlds and entertain visitors from them, you will hear about it sooner or later anyway. I would rather you heard it from a friend. It is a factor you should have in mind to make a better decision on the proposition you have been offered. I think we owe you that much."

"My Cheshire cat . . ." I began.

"Was a Whillowhim," he said, "a representative of one of the most powerful cultures in the galaxy. Competition among the various peoples who make up the total of civilization has always been keen in terms of trade and the exploitation of new worlds. There are great cultures and massive power blocs, and then there are—developing worlds, shall we say?—such as your own, newly arrived at the threshold of the big world. One day your people will probably have membership in our Council, with the right to a voice and a vote. What sort of strength do you think you will wield?"

"Not a whole big hell of a lot," I said.

"And what does one do under such circumstances?"

"Seek alliances, make deals. Look for someone else with common problems and interests."

"You might ally yourself with one of the big power blocs. They would do handsome things for your people in return for your support."

"There would seem a danger of becoming a puppet. Of losing a lot on something like that."

"Perhaps, perhaps not. It is not so simple a thing to foresee. On the other paw, you might throw in with the other smaller groups whose situations are, as you said, similar to you own. There are dangers in that, too, of course, but then the choices are never really this clear-cut. Do you begin to see what I am getting at, though?"

"Possibly. Are there many . . . developing worlds . . . such as my own?"

"Yes," he said. "There is quite a crop of them. New ones keep turning up all the time. A good thing, too—for everybody. We need that diversity—all those viewpoints and unique approaches to the problems life serves up wherever it occurs."

"Am I safe in assuming that a significant number of the younger ones stick together on major issues?"

"You are safe in assuming that."

"Is there a sufficient number to really swing much weight?"

"It is beginning to get to that point."

"I see," I said.

"Yes. Some of the older, more entrenched powers would not mind limiting their force. Curtailing their number is one way to go about it."

"If we had messed up badly with the artifacts, would it have kept us out permanently?"

"Permanently, no. You exist. You are sufficiently developed. You would have to be recognized sooner or later, even if you were blackballed initially. Still, it would be a mark against you, and it would necessarily be later for you then. It would delay things for a long while."

"Did you suspect the Whillowhim all along?"

"I suspected one of the major powers. There have been a number of incidents of this sort—which is why we keep an eye on beginners. In your case, it was easy for them—finding a ready-made situation that might be exploited. Actually, though, I guessed wrong as to who was behind it. I did not really know until that night at the hall when Speicus got his message across and you pursued the Whillowhim. Not that it matters now. If we presented our findings to them and requested an explanation—which we will not do—the Whillowhim would of course simply reply that their agent was not their agent but a private individual of unbalanced nature acting without sanction, and they would regret the inconvenience he had caused. No. Their awareness of failure will be sufficient. We've scotched them here. They know that we are on the job and that you are alert—as your officials now are. I doubt that you will ever be faced with anything this overt in the future."

"I suppose that the next time they will come bearing gifts."

"This is quite likely. But again, your people are now advised. Others will come, too. It should not be so difficult to balance them off against one another."

"So it still comes back to the smoke-filled room . . ."

"Or methane. Or many other things," he said. "I don't quite follow . . ."

"Politics. It's a gas, too."

"Oh, yes. One of life's little essentials."

"Ragma, I would like to ask you a personal question."

"You may. If it is too embarrassing I will simply not answer it."

"Then tell me, if you would, how you would characterize your own culture, race, people—whatever term your social scientists apply to your group, you know what I mean—in terms of the greater galactic civilization."

"Oh, we would call ourselves quite practical, efficient, flat-headed—"

"Level-headed," I said.

208

"Just so. And at the same time idealistic, inventive, full of cultural diversity and—"

I coughed.

"—and possessed of great potential," he said, "and the dreams and vigor of youth."

"Thank you."

We turned and began walking, then, along the beach just out of reach of the tide.

"Have you been thinking about the proposal?" he finally asked.

"Yes," I said.

"Reach a decision yet?"

"No," I said. "I am going to go away for a while to think about it."

"Have you any idea as to how long it will take you?"

"No."

"Just so. Just so. You will of course notify us immediately, whichever you decide . . ."

"Of course."

We passed a faded NO SWIMMING sign, and I paused to reflect on the improvement over the GNIMMIWS ON one I would have seen earlier. My scar collection was back in place too, and cigarettes tasted normal once more. I would miss the backward versions of the soggy French fries, greasy hamburgs, day-old salads and Student Union coffee, though, I decided. Most of all, however, the memory of the stereoisobooze, mystic nectar, *Spiegelschnapps* would haunt me, like a breeze from the stills of Faerie . . .

"I guess we had better be getting back into town," Ragma said. "Merimee's party will be starting soon."

"True," I said. "But tell me something. I was just thinking about inversions that proceed as far as the molecular level but stop short of the atomic, the subatomic . . ."

"And you want to know why the inverter does not deliver neat little piles of antimatter for you?"

"Well, yes."

He shrugged.

"It can be done, but you lose a lot of machines that way, among other things. And this one is an antique. We want to hang onto it. It is the second N-axial inversion until ever built."

"What happened to the first one?"

He chuckled.

"It did not possess a particle-exceptor program."

"How does that work?"

He shook his head.

"There are some things that man is not meant to know," he said.

"That's a hell of a thing to say at this stage of the game."

"Actually, I don't understand it myself."

"Oh."

"Let's go drink Merimee's booze and smoke his cigarettes," he said. "I want to talk to your uncle some more, too. He has offered me a job, you know."

"He has? Doing what?"

"He has some interesting ideas concerning galactic trade. He says that he wants to set up a modest export-import business. You see, I am about ready to retire from the force, and he wants someone with my sort of experience to advise him. We might work something out."

"He is my favorite uncle," I said, "and I owe him a lot. But I am also sufficiently indebted to you that I feel obligated to point out that his reputation is somewhat less than savory."

Ragma shrugged.

"The galaxy is a big place," he said. "There are laws and occasions for all sorts and situations. These are some of the things he wants me to advise him about."

I nodded slowly, apocalyptic pieces of family folklore having but recently fallen into place in light of Merimee's revelations and some of Uncle Albert's own reminiscences during our small family reunion the previous evening.

"Doctor Merimee, by the way, will be a partner in the enterprise," Ragma added.

I continued to nod.

"Whatever happens," I said, "I am certain that you will find it a stimulating and enlightening experience."

We continued to the car, into it, cityward, away. Behind me the beach was suddenly full of doorways, and I thought of ladies, tigers, shoes, ships, sealing wax and other lurkers on the threshold. Soon, soon, soon . . .

Variations on a Theme by the Third Gargoyle from the End: Stars and the Dream of Time—

It was in a small town in the shadow of the Alps that I finally caught up with him, brooding atop the local house of worship, regarding the huge clock high up on the city hall across the way.

"Good evening, Professor Dobson."

"Eh? Fred? Goodness! Mind the next stone over—the mortar is a bit crumbly . . . There. Very good. I hardly expected to see you tonight. Glad you happened by, though. I was going to send you a postcard in the morning, telling you about this place. Not just the climbing but the perspective. Keep your eye on the big clock, will you?"

"All right," I said, settling back onto a perch and bracing one foot against an ornamental projection.

"I've brought you something," I said, passing him the package.

"Why, thank you. Most unexpected. A surprise . . . It gurgles, Fred."

"So it does."

He peeled away the paper.

"Indeed! I can't make out the label, so I had better sample it."

I watched the big clock on the tower.

After a moment, "Fred!" he said. "I've never tasted the like! What is it?"

"The stereoisomer of a common bourbon," I said. "I was permitted to run a few bottles through the Rhennius machine recently, as the UN Special Committee on Alien Artifacts is being particularly nice to me these days. So, in this sense, you have just sampled a very rare thing."

"I see. Yes . . . What is the occasion?"

"The stars have run their fiery courses to their proper places, positioned with elegant cunning, possessed of noble portent."

He nodded.

"Beautifully stated," he said. "But what do you mean?"

"To begin with a departure, I have graduated."

"I am sorry to hear that. I was beginning to believe they would never get you."

"So was I. But they did. I am now working for the State Department or the United Nations, depending on how one looks at these matters."

"What sort of position is it?"

"That is what I am thinking about at the moment. You see, I have a choice."

He took another sip and passed me the bottle.

"Always an awesome moment," he reflected. "Here."

I nodded. I took a sip.

"Which is why I wanted to talk with you before I made it."

"Always an awesome responsibility," he said, recovering the bottle. "Why me?"

"Some time ago, when I was being tormented in the desert," I said, "I thought about the many advisers I have had. It only recently occurred to me what made some of them better than others. The best ones, I see now, were those who did not try to

212

force me to go the prescribed routes. They did not simply sign my card either, though. They always talked to me for a time. Not the usual sort of thing. They never counseled me in the direct manner ritual prescribes for such occasions. I don't even remember much of what was said. Things they had learned the hard way usually, things they considered important, I guess. Generally non-academic things. Those were the ones who taught me something, and perhaps they did direct me in an indirect way. Not to do what they wanted but to see something they had really seen. A piece of their slant on life, take it for whatever it is worth. Anyhow, while you are one of the few who escaped the formal assignment, over the years I have come to consider you my only real adviser."

"It was never intentional . . ." he said.

"Exactly. That was the best way to do it in my case. The only way, probably. You have shown me things that have helped me. Often. Now I am thinking particularly of our recent conversation, back on campus, right before you retired."

"I remember it well."

I lit a cigarette.

"The entire situation is rather difficult to explain," I said. "I will try to simplify it: The star-stone, that alien artifact we have on loan, is sentient. It was created by a now extinct race somewhat similar to our own. It was located among the ruins of their civilization ages after its passing, and no one recognized it for what it was. This is not especially strange, because there was nothing to distinguish it as the Speicus referred to in some of the writings which survived and were subsequently translated. It was assumed that the references indicated some sort of investigating committee or some process or program employed in the gathering and evaluation of information in the area of the social sciences. But it was the star-stone they were talking about. To function properly, it requires a host built along our lines. It exists then as a symbiote within that creature, obtaining data by means of that being's nervous system as it goes about its business. It operates on this material as something of a sociological computer. In return for this, it keeps its host in good repair indefinitely. On request, it provides analyses of anything it has encountered directly or peripherally, along with reliability figures, unbiased because it is uniquely alien to all life forms, yet creature-oriented because of the nature of the input mechanism. It prefers a mobile host with a fact-filled head."

"Fascinating. How did you learn all this?"

"By accident, I partially activated it. It got inside me then and persuaded me to bring it to full function. Which I did. In the process, however, I rendered myself incapable of all but the most rudimentary communication with it. Later, it was removed and I was returned to normal. It is currently functioning, though, and telepathic analysts are capable of conversing with it. Now, both the galactic Council and the United Nations would like to see it employed once more. What has been proposed is that it continue as a special item in the kula chain setup, providing each world it visits with a full report on itself. Moving on, over the years, across the generations, this base would be broadened. Eventually, it would be able to supply the Council with reports encompassing whole sectors of the civilized galaxy. It is a living data processor, mildly telepathic—for it has been absorbing bits and pieces over the centuries it has been circulating, so that it knew to advise me on the Galactic Code and knew of the function of a certain machine. It represents a unique combination of objectivity and empathy, and because of this its reports should be of more than a little value."

"I begin to see the situation," he said.

"Yes. Speicus seems to have taken a liking to me, wants me to do the honors."

"An enormous opportunity."

"True. If I decline, though, I will still get to study many of these things as an alien culture specialist right here on earth."

"Why should you settle for that when you can have the other?"

"I got to thinking about the petty pace, then the acceleration. A while ago we were there, now we are here. Everything in between is a bit unreal—the time between the tops of our towers. Up here, looking down, looking back, I notice for the first time that my towertops are coming closer and closer together. There is a noticeable increase in the tempo of time and the times. Everything down there, between, grows more and more frantic, absurd. You told me that when I finally thought of it I should remember the brandy."

"Yes, I did. Here."

I disposed of my cigarette. I remembered the brandy, drank to it.

"If the distance were not so great you could spit into the face of Time," he observed as I passed it back. "Yes, I did say all that, and it was true at the time. For me."

"And where is it taking us?" I said. "To the top of a particularly tricky spire which we already know to have been long occupied by others. They consider us a developing world, you know—primitive, barbaric. They are most likely right, too. Let's face it. We've been beaten to the top. If I take the job, I will be more of a display item than Speicus."

"Speaking statistically," he said, "it was unlikely that we would be at the top of the heap, just as it is also unlikely that we are at the bottom. I believed everything that I said when I said it and some of it still. But you must remember the circumstances. I was speaking from the end of a career, not the beginning, and I spoke at a moment when one is preoccupied with such matters. There are other thoughts I have entertained since then. Many of them. Such as Professor Kuhn's notions on the structure of scientific revolutions—that a big new idea comes along and shatters traditional patterns of thought, that everything is then put together again from the ground up. Petty pace, bit by bit. After a time, things begin looking tidy once more, except for a few odd scraps and pieces. Then someone throws another brick through the window. It has always been this way for us, and in recent years the bricks have been coming closer and closer together. Not quite as much time for the cleaning up. Then we met the aliens and a whole truckload of bricks arrived. Naturally the intellect is staggered. Whatever we are, though, we are different from anyone else out there. We have to be. No two people or peoples are alike. If for no other reason than this, I know we have something to contribute. It remains to be found, but it must be found. We must survive the current brick-storm, for it is obvious now that others have done it. If we cannot, then we do not deserve to survive and take our place among them. It was not wrong of me to wish to be the first and the best, only perhaps wrong to wish to be alone. The trouble with you people in anthropology, for all your talk of cultural relativism, is that the very act of evaluation automatically makes you feel superior to whatever you are evaluating, and you evaluate everything. We are now about to be evaluees for a time, anthropologists included. I suspect that has hit you harder than you may be willing to admit, in your favorite area of thought. I would then say, bear up and learn something from it. Humility, if nothing else. We are on the threshold of a renaissance if I read the signs right. But one day the brick-fall will probably let up and Time will shuffle its feet and the sweeping of the floors will commence again. There will be opportunity to feel alone in ourselves once more. When that day comes for you, what sort of company will you have?"

He paused. Then: "You have come for my advice," he said, "and I have probably offered more than was wanted. I owe it to the good company and the perfect beverage. So I drink to you now and to the time that has transfigured me. Keep climbing. That is all. Keep climbing, and then go a little higher."

I accepted a sip. I stared out at the building across the way. I lit another cigarette.

"Why are we watching the clock?" I asked.

"For the chimes at midnight. Any moment now, I should think."

"It seems an awfully obvious moral, even if it is well timed."

He chuckled.

"I didn't script the thing," he said, "and I've used up all my morals, Fred. I just want to enjoy the spectacle. Things can be interesting in themselves."

"True. Sorry. Also, thank you."

"Here they come!" he said.

A little door on either side of the clock popped open. From the one a burnished knight emerged. From the other, a dusky fool. The one bore a sword, the other a staff. They advanced, the knight straight and stately, the fool with a skip or a limp—I was not certain which. They moved toward us, bobbing, frozen in frown and grin. They reached the ends of their tracks, pivoted ninety degrees and proceeded once more to a meeting before a bell that occupied a central position on that lateral way. Arriving before it, the knight raised his weapon and delivered the first blow. The sound was full and deep. Moments later, the fool swung his staff for the second. The tone was slightly sharper, the volume about the same.

Knight, fool, knight, fool . . . The strokes came quite smartly at that range, so I felt them as well as hearing their tones. Fool, knight, fool, knight . . . They cut the air, they killed the day. The fool delivered the final blow.

For an instant, then, they seemed to regard each other. Then, as by agreement, they turned away, moved back to their corners, pivoted, continued to their doorways and entered. The doors closed behind them and even the echoes were dead by then.

"People who don't climb cathedrals miss some good shows," I said.

"Keep your damn morals for another day," he said. Then: "To the lady with the smile!"

"To the rocks of empire!" I replied moments later.

Bits & Pieces Lost in Hilbert Space, Emerging to Describe Slow Symphonies & the Architecture of Persistent Passion—

He regards the night as he had never seen it before, from atop the high Tower of Cheslerei in a place called Ardel beside the sea with the cryptic name. Somewhere, Paul Byler is chipping pieces off a world and doing remarkable things with them. Ira Enterprises, under the directorship of Albert Cassidy, is about to open offices on fourteen planets. A book called *The Retching of the Spirit,* by a shadowy, Traven-like author who lists as collaborators a girl, a dwarf and a donkey, has just achieved best-seller status. *La Gioconda* continues to receive critical acclaim with tacit good humor and traditional poise. Dennis Wexroth is on crutches as the result of a broken leg sustained while attempting to scale the Student Union.

He thinks of these and many other things behind the sky, within it. He recalls his departure.

Charv had said, "You smoke too much, you know. Perhaps you can cut down on this trip, or quit entirely. At any rate, have a lot of good, clean fun. Along with hard, honest work, it makes the worlds go round."

Nadler had shaken his hand firmly, smiled perfectly and said, "I know you will always be a credit to the corps, Doctor Cassidy.

When in doubt invoke tradition and improvise. Always remember what you represent."

Merimee had winked and said, "We'll be opening a string of cat houses around the galaxy, for traveling earthmen and adventuresome extees. It won't be long. Cultivate philosophy in the meantime. And if you get in any trouble, remember my number."

"Fred, my boy," his uncle had said, flipping his blackthorn aside to squeeze his shoulders, "this is a great day for the Cassidys! I always knew that you would meet your fate somewhere among the stars above. Second sight, you know. Godspeed, and a copy of Tom Moore here for company. I'll be in touch about the Vibesper office and maybe be sending Ragma along later. You've been a proud investment, boy!"

He smiles at the absurdity, the traditions, the intentions. He feels the emotions.

I am sorry about that spasm back on the bus, Fred. It was just that I was trying to learn how your body worked in case I had to do any repairs. I was handicapped by the handedness barrier.

"I guessed as much—later."

This world is an interesting place, Fred. We have been here only a day and I can already predict, with high reliability, that we are going to have some unusual experiences.

"What sort of satisfaction do you get out of all this, Speicus?"

I am a recording and analyzing device. The best comparison, I suppose, is that I am a combination of the tourist and his camera. At those moments when they function together, I imagine that their sensations are akin to my own.

"I suppose it feels good to know yourself so thoroughly. I doubt that I ever will."

He lights a cigarette. He gestures.

"Well, was it worth the trip?" he asks.

You already know the answer to that.

"Yes, I guess that I do."

The people who climbed up and decorated all those rocks and cave walls had the right idea, he decides. Yes, they did.

Why he decides this I am not certain. I know him well, of course. But I doubt that I will ever know him thoroughly either. I am a recording . . .

Also Available

All is not what it seems . . .

In the murky London gloom, a knife-wielding gentleman named Jack prowls the midnight streets with his faithful watch-dog Snuff – gathering together the grisly ingredients they will need for an upcoming ancient and unearthly rite. For soon after the death of the moon, black magic will summon the Elder Gods back into the world. And all manner of Players, both human and undead, are preparing to participate.

Some have come to open the gates. Some have come to slam them shut.

And now the dread night approaches – so let the Game begin.

"Sparkling, witty, delightful. Zelazny's best for ages, perhaps his best ever." *Kirkus Reviews*

OUT NOW!

About the Author

Roger Zelazny (1937-1995) is one of the most celebrated names in SF and fantasy. During his lifetime he was honoured with numerous prizes, including six Hugo and three Nebula Awards. He wrote more than fifty books, including the Amber novels, *Lord of Light,* and *A Night in the Lonesome October.*

Note from the Publisher

We occasionally send newsletters with details of new releases, special offers and other book news.

Join the Farrago Readers Group now, for more on Roger Zelazny - and other comparable authors to make you smile!

Sign up here: farragobooks.com/zelazny-signup